High Elk's Treasure

Virginia Driving Hawk Sneve

WITH RELATED READINGS

THE EMC MASTERPIECE SERIES

Access Editions

EMC/Paradigm Publishing
St. Paul, Minnesota

Staff Credits:

Laurie Skiba
Managing Editor

Paul Spencer
Art and Photo Researcher

Brenda Owens
High School Editor

Valerie Murphy
Editorial Assistant

Becky Palmer
Associate Editor

Sharon O'Donnell
Copy Editor

Nichola Torbett
Associate Editor

Shelley Clubb
Production Manager

Jennifer Anderson
Assistant Editor

Jennifer Wreisner
Senior Designer

Lori Coleman
Editorial Consultant

Parkwood Composition
Compositor

Sneve, Virginia Driving Hawk.
    High elk's treasure / Virginia Driving Hawk Sneve.
    p. cm. – (The EMC masterpiece series access editions)
Includes plot analysis, related readings, activities, and projects.
Summary: Trying to locate a valuable filly lost during a storm, thirteen-year-old Joe High Elk discovers an object of historical importance.
    ISBN 0-8219-2414-1
    1. Dakota Indians—Juvenile fiction. [1.Dakota Indians—Fiction. 2. Indians of North America—Great Plains—Fiction.] I. Title. II. Series.

PZ7.S679 Hi 2002
[Fic]—dc21

2001055673

ISBN 0-8219-2414-1

Published by EMC/Paradigm Publishing
875 Montreal Way
St. Paul, Minnesota 55102
800-328-1452
www.emcp.com
E-mail: educate@emcp.com

Printed in the United States of America.
1 2 3 4 5 6 7 8 9 10 xxx 12 11 10 09 08 07 06 05 04 03

Table of Contents

Virginia Driving Hawk Sneve

Virginia Driving Hawk Sneve[1] (b.1933) is an award-winning author who writes stories, poems, and novels about Native American life. She was born on the Rosebud Indian Reservation in South Dakota on February 21, 1933. That same year, her father, James Driving Hawk, finished divinity school and became a priest at All Saints Episcopal Chapel in Milk's Camp at Ponca Creek, South Dakota. Her mother, Rose Ross Posey, was an active member of the Rosebud Sioux tribe. To support the family, Virginia's parents often worked at extra jobs that were far away from the reservation. One summer, her parents worked in Sioux Falls, her mother as a hotel maid and her father at a meat packing company. While their parents were at work, Virginia and her brother Edward spent a lot of time with their grandmothers. Both grandmothers, Flora Clairmont Driving Hawk and Hannah Howe Frazier, loved to tell Virginia about her ancestors. Virginia learned that she was a mixture of several heritages: three Dakota tribes, Santee, Teton, and Yankton; Ponca, a tribe with origins in Nebraska; French; Scottish; and English.

Virginia attended elementary school on the Rosebud reservation. Her first teacher, Mr. Miller, encouraged her to read and lent her books from his own personal library. Virginia also read *The Book of Knowledge*. "It was the usual encyclopedia, but it also had selections of classic mythology and literature, plus what is now called 'hands on' activities," she said. "I read and reread all twenty volumes. I was heartbroken when we had to leave them behind when we again moved. Years later as an adult, I found the same set at an estate sale and bought it. I still enjoy browsing through the stories."

During World War II (1939–1945), Virginia's father tried to enlist as a soldier but was rejected because of stomach problems. Instead he continued with his ministry. He also considered his children's educations to be very important. During a snowstorm one year, he

---

1. **Sneve.** Pronounced snā´vē

carried Virginia to school on his back because he did not want her to miss even a day of school. After World War II, Virginia was sent away to attend high school at St. Mary's School for Indian Girls in Springfield, South Dakota. During this time, most Native American young people who wanted to continue their educations were sent to boarding schools because there were no high schools on reservations. Alhough Virginia was able to take piano and organ lessons and her teachers encouraged her writing talent, she missed her family greatly. Virginia's father died of stomach cancer two years before she graduated from high school in 1950.

After high school, Virginia attended South Dakota State College in Brookings, South Dakota. She earned a bachelor's degree in English and history in 1954 and began teaching music and English at White Public High School and Pierre Junior High School. Later Virginia taught English, speech, and drama at Flandreau Indian School. She received a master's degree in education and guidance from South Dakota State University in 1969. In 1988, Virginia taught at both Oglala Lakota College and Rapid City Central High School.

Virginia married Vance Sneve, a Bureau of Indian Affairs employee. Together they raised three children who called themselves "Siouxwegians" because their father was Norwegian and their mother was a Lakota. Virginia Driving Hawk Sneve, like her own mother and father, encouraged her children to read. When she discovered that most books for young children did not provide realistic portrayals of Native Americans, Sneve decided to write books for children. She wrote stories that gave a realistic portrayal of Native American life and traditions, and she based her stories on her own experiences.

Today Sneve is the author of more than twenty books and has written novels, poetry books, histories, and biographies. She published her first books, *Betrayed, Jimmy Yellow Hawk,* and *High Elk's Treasure,* in 1972. In 1995 Sneve wrote *Completing the Circle,* which included historical accounts of the lives of her grandmothers and great-grandmothers. In 2000 she wrote *Grandpa Was a Cowboy and an Indian and Other Stories,* a collection of Lakota folklore and stories based on historical events.

Sneve has won many awards for her writing. In 1979 she received an honorary doctorate from Dakota Wesleyan University in Mitchell, South Dakota. She has also received the Writer of the Year Award, the South Dakota Education Association Human Services Award, the Spirit of Crazy Horse Award, the Author-Illustrator Human and Civil Rights Award, the South Dakota State Counselors' Association Human Rights Award, and the Living Indian Artist Treasure Award. Perhaps Sneve's most prestigious award came in 2000 when she received the National Humanities Medal from President Bill Clinton. According to National Endowment for the Humanities Chairman William R. Ferris, "National Humanities Medalists are distinguished individuals who have made extraordinary contributions to American cultural life and thought." Other Americans who have received this award include humorist Garrison Keillor, musicians Don Henley and Quincy Jones, filmmaker Steven Spielberg, and author Toni Morrison. Today, Virginia Driving Hawk Sneve continues to write and speak about Native American culture and life.

BOOKS BY VIRGINIA DRIVING HAWK SNEVE

Betrayed

ChiChi HooHoo Bogeyman

Completing the Circle

Dancing Teepees: Poems of American Indian Youth

Enduring Wisdom: Sayings from American Indians

Grandpa Was a Cowboy and an Indian and Other Stories

High Elk's Treasure

Holiday House First Americans Series (a series of books that describe the history and culture of several Native North American nations)

Jimmy Yellow Hawk

South Dakota Geographic Names

That They May Have Life: The Episcopal Church in South Dakota

They Led a Nation

The Trickster and the Troll

When Thunders Spoke

Time Line of Virginia Driving Hawk Sneve's Life

1933	Virginia Driving Hawk is born on February 21, 1933, on the Rosebud Indian Reservation near Mission, South Dakota.
1935	Virginia's brother Edward is born.
1936	Virginia's parents find seasonal jobs off the reservation to supplement her father's income.
1938	Virginia begins school at Milk's Camp Bureau of Indian Affairs Day School.
1939	World War II begins.
1940	Virginia moves to a church with a library that contains *The Book of Knowledge,* an encyclopedia that greatly influenced her.
1944	Virginia's father tries to enlist in the army and the marines. He is rejected by both because of a stomach problem.
1946	Virginia begins St. Mary's High School for Indian Girls in Springfield, South Dakota.
1948	Virginia's father dies in May in Yankton, South Dakota.
1950	Virginia graduates from high school and goes to South Dakota State College in Brookings, South Dakota.
1954	Virginia earns a bachelor's degree in English and history from South Dakota State College.
1954–1969	Virginia teaches music and English at White Public High School and Pierre Junior High School. Virginia also teaches English, speech, and drama and is a counselor at Flandreau Indian School. Virginia marries Vance M. Sneve, a Bureau of Indian Affairs employee.
1969	Virginia Driving Hawk Sneve receives a master's degree in education and guidance from South Dakota State University.
1972	Sneve writes her first books, *Betrayed, Jimmy Yellow Hawk,* and *High Elk's Treasure.* All are based on stories told by her grandmothers.
1973	Sneve completes *South Dakota Geographic Names.*
1974	Sneve writes *When Thunders Spoke,* the story of a fifteen-year-old boy who finds a sacred stick that can make unusual things happen.
1975	Sneve writes two more books, *ChiChi HooHoo Bogeyman,* the story of three young cousins who find the real bogeyman, and *They Led a Nation,* a collection of biographies of twenty Dakota leaders.
1977	*That They May Have Life,* a history of the Episcopal Church in South Dakota from 1859 to 1976, is published.
1979	Sneve receives an honorary doctorate of letters from Dakota Wesleyan University in Mitchell, South Dakota.

The Western Heritage Hall of Fame presents Sneve with the Writer of the Year Award.

1984

Sneve is an associate instructor of English at Oglala Lakota College and a guidance counselor at Rapid City Central High School.

1988

Dancing Teepees: Poems of American Indian Youth is published.

1989

Sneve receives the South Dakota Education Association Human Services Award.

1994

In June, Sneve retires from her teaching positions.

1995

The University of Nebraska gives Sneve the Native American Prose Award for *Completing the Circle,* a biography of Dakota and Ponca women.

1995

Sneve receives the Spirit of Crazy Horse Award from Black Hills Seminars' Youth at Risk, the Author-Illustrator Human and Civil Rights Award from the National Education Association, and the South Dakota State Counselors' Association Human Rights Award.

1996

Sneve writes *The Trickster and the Troll.* She is also presented the Living Indian Artist Treasure Award by the Northern Plains Tribal Arts and South Dakotans for the Arts.

1997

Sneve writes *Enduring Wisdom: Sayings from American Indians* and *Grandpa Was a Cowboy and an Indian and Other Stories.* She also becomes the first South Dakotan to receive the National Humanities Medal. In December, Sneve receives the award from President Clinton at a ceremony in Constitution Hall in Washington, DC.

2000

American Indians on the Plains

American Indians on the North American Continent

American Indians, or Native Americans, have lived on the North American continent for more than 18,000 years. When Columbus arrived in 1492, approximately sixty million Native Americans lived on the continent. Some of these Native Americans lived in complex urban societies; others, especially those who lived on the plains, developed farming and hunter-gatherer societies, societies that would change greatly with the arrival of the horse.

The Introduction of the Horse

In the early 1500s, Spanish explorers brought horses to present-day New Mexico. When Pueblo Indians forced the Spanish back to Mexico in 1684, many horses were left behind. Although the Pueblos learned to ride these horses, they considered horses to be more valuable as a trade item. They often traded horses to Plains tribes for dried buffalo meat and clothing. Plains nations such as the Dakota, the Cheyenne, and the Crow found horses to be very useful. Although dogs had long been used to pull supply sleds, the introduction of horses made moving about the plains a much simpler task. Horses allowed Plains people to travel longer and go farther in search of food and trade, and they made it easier to capture buffalo and fight off enemies. Horses became extremely important possessions. An American Indian family's wealth and well being was often tied to the number of and quality of the horses they owned. Indeed, in the early 1800s, many Crow families had more than one hundred horses.

The Westward Movement of White Settlers

As the United States began to develop, white settlers began to move farther and farther west searching for farmland. As this westward movement expanded, many Native Americans were pressured to stay ahead of the white settlers. Tribes in the Ojibwa and Sioux nations moved from east coast locations to Midwest locations near the Mississippi River Valley. *Sioux*, a shortened form of *Nadowessioux*—which means "little snakes"—was a name given to certain Plains tribes by enemy tribes. What Americans and the French called Sioux at that time, were actually a collection of several tribes. By the early 1800s, the nation then known as the Sioux was one of the largest and most powerful Indian nations in the United States. Today, the Sioux prefer to be called Dakota, Lakota, or Nakota, according to the dialect spoken by their native group. The eastern Sioux, or Santee, speak Dakota; the western Sioux, or Tetons, speak Lakota; and the Yankton Sioux speak Nakota.

The Fort Laramie Treaties

In 1851 and 1868, Plains Indians such as the Cheyenne, Crow, Arapaho, and Sioux signed treaties at Fort Laramie, Wyoming. The treaties allowed roads to cross Native American lands. Native Americans who signed the treaties agreed to stay away from trails used by white settlers moving west. In return, the Native Americans received food, money, supplies, and a guarantee of hunting rights on land in more remote locations. The 1868 Fort Laramie Treaty named the Black Hills area of South Dakota as a part of the Great Sioux Reservation.

The Battle of Little Big Horn

In 1874, gold was discovered in the Black Hills. As settlers and miners flocked west, bands of American Indians often attacked travelers looking for gold or new land. To protect the travelers, the United States government sent troops to fight and kill American Indians who were hindering, or slowing, westward movement.

One of the largest battles fought between government troops and American Indians occurred in 1876 in what is now Montana. Thousands of Sioux, Cheyenne, and Arapaho had gathered at a village called Little Big Horn (or the Greasy Grass) for an annual buffalo hunt. On June 25, government troops led by Lieutenant Colonel George Custer attacked the Native Americans gathered there. The Native Americans fought back and killed Custer and all of his men.

After the loss at the Battle of Little Big Horn, the United States government sent additional troops to fight. Many tribal leaders were arrested or killed. The Black Hills area was given back to the federal government. By the late-1800s, many hungry and defeated American Indians signed treaties with the federal government.

The Allotment Act

The Allotment Act, also known as the Dawes Severalty Act, was passed by Congress in 1887. Native American lands were divided into allotments, or pieces of land, to encourage Indian people to stop wandering the plains and become farmers. Most Native American families received allotments of 160 acres per family. Leftover land not allotted to Native Americans was sold to whites. Native Americans were also allowed to sell their allotments. By 1933, 80 million acres of Native American land had been sold to white settlers.

The Great Sioux Reservation

In 1889, the United States Congress split the Great Sioux Reservation into six smaller reservations. Those who were labeled Sioux were forced onto these reservations. Some were forced to travel great distances, far away from lands they had previously lived on. Others had to join with groups of people whose beliefs were not similar to their own. All had to change their entire way of life.

Today, Dakota, Lakota, and Nakota populations on the reservations are still changing as Indian people work to preserve native languages and customs. Reservations such as the Rosebud, Cheyenne River, Pine Ridge, Standing Rock, Lower Brule, Crow Creek, Lake Traverse, Yankton, and Flandreau are involved in a wide variety of social, economic, and cultural activities.

The Rise of American Indian Influence

In 1910 the total Native American population in North America had fallen to its lowest ever—250,000. The 1920s saw American Indians gain more control over their lives. In 1924 all Native Americans were granted citizenship. In 1934 the Indian Reorganization Act stopped the allotment process and gave money to reservations for the development of their resources. During World War II, many Native Americans helped with the war effort at home and abroad. After the war, many Native Americans settled in large cities and worked to regain more power in American society.

Native Americans Today

Only 35 percent of American Indians in the United States still live on reservations. Approximately 300 reservations remain, varying in size from small ranches in California to the 14-million-acre Navajo reservation that covers parts of Arizona, New Mexico, and Utah. Reservations vary greatly in their economic status. Some have large populations that live in poverty and face high unemployment. Other tribes are doing well and operate gambling casinos, sell arts and crafts, and explore other industries. Their numbers are on the rise again, at more than two million and growing.

Native Americans today are actors, singers, doctors, teachers, and lawmakers. On and off the reservation, they are working hard to preserve their languages and cultures. At the same time, they want to end stereotypes others may have about how they live and think. Like other groups of Americans, they are diverse and hold many different views on major issues such as education, religion, and politics.

Characters in *High Elk's Treasure*

Major Characters

Joe High Elk (Joe). Joe is the protagonist, or main character, in the novel. He is thirteen and an eighth-grade student at a reservation elementary school. In this novel Joe is tested by several new and difficult situations. Although he sometimes loses his temper, he handles most situations well. Joe loves his family and he loves horses. He is also proud of his heritage. His great-grandfather once owned huge herds of beautiful, strong horses. Joe would like to rebuild his great-grandfather's herd.

William High Elk (Will). William High Elk is Joe High Elk's father. He works for the Bureau of Indian Affairs. William and his family live on the reservation two miles from the main road. William wants to rebuild High Elk's horse herd, but he does not have enough money to buy more horses. He is a kind and understanding father.

Albert Blue Shield (Mr. Blue Shield). Mr. Blue Shield's family lives on land next to the High Elks' land. He is a kind and helpful neighbor. He helps the High Elks tackle several difficult problems that arise in the novel. He also befriends Howard Anderson.

Howard Anderson (Howard Pretty Flute). Howard Anderson is related to the High Elks. His grandfather and Joe's grandfather were brothers. He ran away from home when he had trouble adjusting to a new school. He gets into trouble, but eventually he does the right things. If he had stayed in school, he would have been a senior in high school. He cares about his mother and stepfather and feels sorry that he has disappointed them.

Minor Characters

Mr. Gray Bear. Mr. Gray Bear teaches seventh and eighth graders at an elementary day school on a reservation. He has a close relationship with his students and cares about their daily lives.

Marie. Ten-year-old Marie is Joe's sister. She is small for her age and becomes anxious in the face of danger. She loves her family and also wants to see the High Elk herd rebuilt.

Grandma High Elk. Grandma High Elk, Joe's grandmother, can speak English but speaks mostly Lakota. She knows a lot about the High Elk family history. She is superstitious and is afraid to talk about some things that happened to her father, High Elk.

High Elk. High Elk is Joe's great-grandfather. He is now dead. He once had a huge herd of horses, but when the market went bad in the 1920s, he lost most of his herd. High Elk was present at the Battle of Little Big Horn. After the battle, his mother's illness forced him to move to the reservation. He and his sons received allotments of land from the federal government. Some of this land was later sold to the government. The rest is still High Elk land.

Šungwiye. Šungwiye is the last remaining horse from High Elk's herd. Šungwiye is the mother of Star and is about to give birth to another foal.

Marlene High Elk. Marlene is Joe's mother. She works for the Bureau of Indian Affairs.

Star. Star is a filly, or young female horse, owned by Joe High Elk's family. Though only a minor character, Star is part of the major action in the story. Star's mother, Šungwiye, is the last remaining horse of High Elk's once-large herd.

Mrs. Blue Shield and the Blue Shield girls. They are the wife and daughters of Mr. Blue Shield and are friends of the High Elks.

Frank Iron Cloud. Frank Iron Cloud is the tribal chairman.

Dr. Scott. Dr. Scott is a historian at the state university. He is a highly analytical man and is excited about acting as an "authoritative witness" for the High Elks.

Martin. Martin is the leader of a band of horse thieves. He is mean and has a record of participating in illegal activities.

Otokahe. Otokahe is Šungwiye's new colt, or male foal. *Otokahe* means "beginning."

Echoes:

The Native American Experience in the 1800s

Every year white intruders become more greedy, exacting, oppressive, and overbearing.

—Tecumseh, Shawnee Chief, in an 1812 speech

The Great Spirit made us, the Indians, and gave us this land we live in. He gave us the buffalo, the antelope, and the deer for food and clothing. We moved our hunting grounds from the Minnesota to the Platte and from the Mississippi to the great mountains. No one put bounds on us. We were free as the winds, and like the eagle, heard no man's commands.

—Red Cloud, in a farewell address to his people on July 4, 1903

I had never seen a Wasichu [white person] then, and did not know what one looked like, but everyone was saying that the Wasichus were coming and that they were going to take our country and rub us out and that we should all have to die fighting.

—Black Elk, describing a December 21, 1866, battle

They say we massacred him [Custer], but he would have done the same thing to us had we not defended ourselves and fought to the last.

—Last words of Crazy Horse in 1877

The Native American Experience Today

I like living in this community, and I like being Choctaw, but that's all there is to it. Just because I don't want to be a white man doesn't mean I want to be some kind of mystical Indian either. Just a real human being.

—Beasley Denson, secretary/treasurer of the Choctaw Tribal Council

. . . I strive to be honest and accurate about the Native American experience portrayed in my work. In so doing, I hope to dispel stereotypes and to show my reading audience that Native Americans have a proud past, a viable present, and a hopeful future.

—Virginia Driving Hawk Sneve, author of *High Elk's Treasure*

It's a good day to be indigenous.

—Line from the 1998 movie, *Smoke Signals*

Remember that you are all people and that all people are you. Remember that you are this universe and that this universe is you.

—from "Remember," a poem by Joy Harjo

Images from Dakota History

Photo: ©CORBIS

An 1865 portrait of George Custer with his brother Tom (standing) and his wife Libby Custer.

Photo: ©CORBIS

Rain-in-the-Face.

Photo: © Dan Lamont/CORBIS

A recent photograph of the town of Rosebud on the Rosebud Indian Reservation in South Dakota.

Critical Viewing

These pictures represent two different views of the Battle of Little Big Horn. What similarities and differences do you see between them? What is the point of view of each? What ideas do you think the makers of each image wanted to communicate?

The Battle of Little Big Horn by Kicking Bear. Kicking Bear, a Lakota warrior, painted his recollection of Little Big Horn in 1898. The four standing figures near the center are Sitting Bull, Rain-in-the-Face, Crazy Horse, and Kicking Bear. Lying below them to the left is the body of George Custer, dressed in buckskin.

This mass-produced print from 1889 was popular among Euro-Americans. Custer is depicted standing in the center.

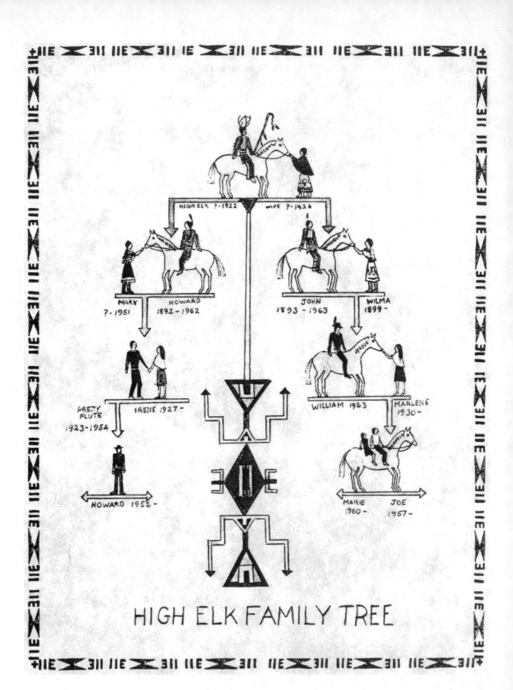

HIGH ELK FAMILY TREE

High Elk's Treasure

Virginia Driving Hawk Sneve

Author's Note

The story, places, and characters in this book are fictitious, with the exception of General Custer, his brother, and the Sioux warrior, Rain-in-the-Face.

The Battle of the Little Big Horn is recorded historically; but the manner of General Custer's death has never been authenticated. I make no claim to any new or specific knowledge of the General's death.

My thanks to my grandmother, Flora Driving Hawk, and to Mr. and Mrs. Emmet Jones for their assistance in the spelling, definition, and pronunciation of Sioux words.

Virginia Driving Hawk Sneve

Glossary with Phonetic Pronunciation

INA *(eeh-nah):* my mother

IYOPTE *(ee-yo-ptay,* the *p* is an exploded sound not found in English): get going

LAKOTA or DAKOTA: what the Sioux called themselves, meaning friendly people

NIYE *(nee-yea):* you

OH HINH: exclamation of shock, surprise or fear. Similar to "Oh dear" in English

OTOKAHE *(oh-toe-kaw-hey):* beginning

PARFLECHE *(par-flesh):* a case made of rawhide with the hair removed

PILAMIYE or PIDAMIYE *(pee-la-me-yea):* thank you

SIOUX *(soo):* Early French settlers first gave the Dakota this name, taken from the Chippewa "Nadowessi" which means poisonous snake, or enemy. The French changed the spelling to "Nadowessioux" which was in time shortened to Sioux.

ŠUNGWIYE *(shoong-we-yea):* mare

TAKOZA *(tah-ko-zha):* grandchild

TÉHINDA *(tay-hin-dah,* the *h* is sounded as in the *ch* of the German "ach"): forbid, taboo

TIPI *(tee-pee):* a cone-shaped tent of animal skins, used by the Plains Indians

TRAVOIS *(tr-voy):* a sledge used by the Plains Indians, consisting of a net or platform dragged along the ground on two poles that support it and serve as shafts for the horse or dog pulling it

UN *(oon,* second person singular of the verb "to be"): are

UNCI *(oon-chee):* my grandmother

WANAǦI *(wah-nah-gee,* the *g* is a gutteral sound not found in English): a ghost

WAŠICUN or WAŠICU *(wah-she-choon):* white man, white woman, white person

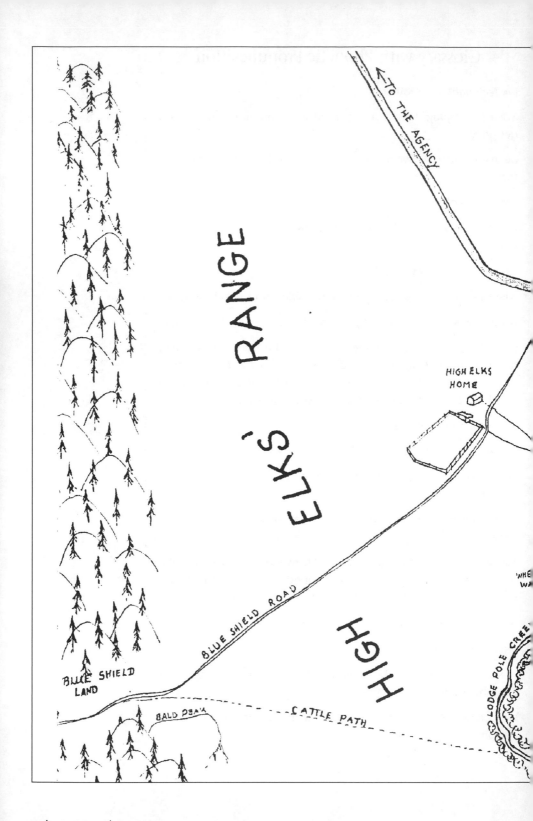

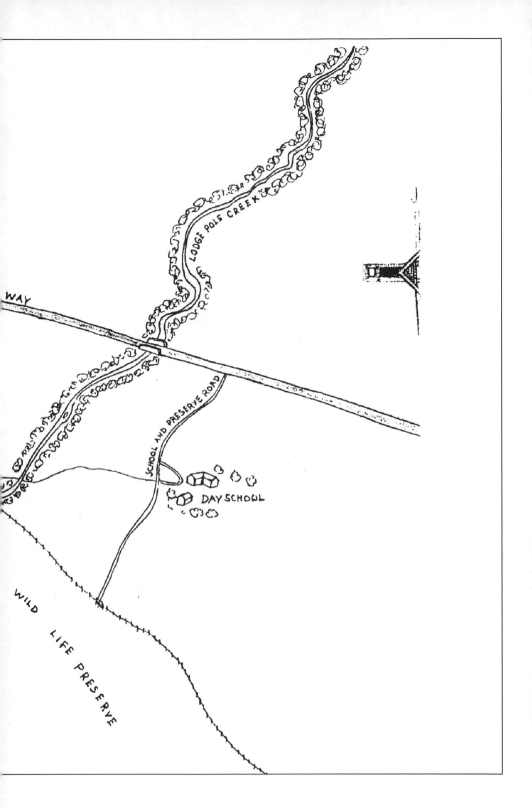

WAY

LODGE POLE CREEK

SCHOOL AND PRESERVE ROAD

DAY SCHOOL

WILD LIFE PRESERVE

MAP **XXV**

OTOKAHE, The Beginning

IN THE AUTUMN of the year 1876, a harried band of Brulé Sioux[1] gave up their freedom and permanently settled on the Dakota reservation[2] which had been set aside for them. They had been part of the huge encampment of Sioux and Cheyenne which had defeated General Custer at the Battle of the Little Big Horn on June 25, 1876. Unable to hunt game, constantly hounded by the United States Army and forced to hide, they came to the hated reservation because they could no longer defend themselves and they were starving.

◀ Why did the Brule Sioux go to the Dakota reservation in 1876?

Among this pitiful little band was a youth called High Elk. He was in the beginning of his manhood, seething with rage at the white men who were destroying his people and who had killed his father. High Elk came only because his mother was ill and _desperately_ needed a place to rest and regain her health. He walked to the reservation, leading an old, scrawny _palomino_ on which his mother rode. The mare was too lame to be ridden far, and was barely able to pull a travois[3] holding their tipi[4] and a few personal belongings.

◀ What did High Elk bring with him?

The mare, her rib and hip bones sharply protruding, was permanently lamed. Her coat was ragged and much of her mane and tail were gone. She didn't look strong enough to pull the travois and she stumbled as she walked. Perhaps this was why the soldiers let High Elk keep her.

High Elk (whose name had originally been Steps-High-Like-An-Elk) loved horses, as did all of the Sioux. Sioux

---

1. **Brulé Sioux.** Group of Native Americans who live in the central plains of the United States
2. **Dakota reservation.** Land in South Dakota set aside by the federal government for the Dakota Indians
3. **travois.** Sledge used by the Plains Indians, consisting of a net or platform dragged along the ground on two poles that support it and serve as shafts for the horse or dog pulling it
4. **tipi.** Cone-shaped tent of animal skins, used by Plains Indians

| **words for everyday use** | des • per • ate (des´pər it) adj., suffering extreme need or anxiety. _The homeless family had a desperate need for a place to spend the night._ **desperately,** adv. | pal • o • mi • no (pal ə mē´nō) n., horse that is pale cream or gold in color and has a flaxen or white mane and tail. _Jessica rode her palomino in the Fourth of July parade._ |

▶ Why were horses important to the Sioux?

horsemen had been the bravest, most daring, and most _agile_ of all the Plains Indians. Horses were the Sioux's wealth and their whole life style was built around the _mobility_ which the animals provided them.

High Elk had plans for his mare and _tethered_ her near the tipi. As the animal grazed bare all of the grass around, he moved the tipi. He had to watch over the mare at all times, for starving Indians might try to steal her for food. Even High Elk's mother felt that the horse should be slaughtered to provide them with meat.

Still High Elk kept the mare. He let no one but himself handle her, and he did dangerous things to ensure her healthy survival. Under the cover of night he would often slip into the agency stables to steal oats for her to eat.

▶ How did High Elk keep his mare alive?

When her strength was revived and she fattened, he sneaked her into the agency corral[5] and bred her to a great, golden quarter horse. This handsome animal belonged to the Agent who was building a herd of golden ponies with choice mares taken from the Indians. If this white man had seen High Elk's mare, now that she was in good condition again, he would have taken the horse in spite of her lame leg. So High Elk used every precaution to hide his treasure.

The mare bore a beautiful filly with the golden color of her sire and the white face and stockings of her dam. The filly thrived, and once more High Elk bred the palomino to the same stud.

As he was sneaking the mare out of the corral the guards discovered him. Thinking that he was trying to steal a horse to eat, they shot at him. Even though High Elk's right leg was shattered, he managed to mount the lame mare and ride safely home. He knew that he dare not stay in the open with a wounded leg since he was now unable to protect his mother or his horses. So High Elk

---

5. **agency corral.** Livestock enclosure on government land

words for everyday use

ag • ile (aʹjəl) _adj._, able to move in a quick and easy fashion. _The agile football player was the first to complete the obstacle course._

mo • bile (mōʹbil) _adj._, capable of moving or being moved. _A motorized wheelchair allows many patients to become more mobile._ **mobility,** _n._

teth • er (teʹthər) _v._, fasten or restrain by or as if by a tether. _My dog couldn't get out of the yard because my mom decided to tether him to a tree._

and his mother moved to the bank of a creek where a large, shallow cave provided shelter and sanctuary for them. The thickly wooded bank concealed the opening of the cave and they remained undiscovered. The mare safely bore a colt and the herd was begun.

In 1887 the federal government passed the General Allotment Act, and High Elk and his mother each received 160 acres of land which bordered the creek on both sides. He was able to take the horses out of hiding. After his mother died, High Elk married. He and his wife had two sons who were alloted 60 acres each. With the additional land High Elk increased the size of his herd. The boys, in their teens, became skilled at capturing the wild mustang mares which High Elk selected to be bred into his herd. High Elk could no longer ride in the hunt, but would supervise from atop the Bald Peak on the Lodge Pole Ridge while his sons chased the wild ponies below.

◀ Where did High Elk get his ranch?

By the time High Elk died, his horses had become famous for their beauty and for their ability to endure the harsh weather of the plains. Their speed and weight were also ideal for ranch work, and High Elk had begun to make money on the sale of his horses.

◀ How did High Elk earn his wealth?

After High Elk's death his two sons quarreled and Howard sold his share of the horses and land and left the reservation. John, the second son, continued to operate the ranch. Then in the 1920's and early 30's the market for horses fell. The herd, the only source of the High Elks' income, decreased. Many of the horses were sold cheaply and others ran with the wild mustangs.

◀ How did the High Elk family lose their wealth?

William, High Elk's grandson, dreamed of rebuilding the herd. He refused to permit farming on land which had never been turned by a plow. William found work as a maintenance man at the agency and was able to support his parents and the one remaining mare, until his father died.

William always hoped someday to buy back the land which had been sold by his uncle, Howard High Elk, but the hope died when most of those acres were turned into a wildlife preserve and the rest used as grounds for the Bureau of Indian Affairs day school. His dreams of rebuilding the herd faded as the expenses grew with his young family. His mother, who lived with them, was an additional drain on his <u>meager</u> resources. There never seemed to be the money to start anew.

The one remaining mare that William raised had become a pet which his children rode to school. Even with just one horse left, William had paid the fee for services of a stud of the same line so that the strain[6] would remain pure. This last remaining mare had borne a filly, and would soon foal again. The High Elks all hoped the new foal would be a male so that the herd would have a fresh beginning.

William's son, thirteen-year-old Joe, had heard the tales of the High Elk horses all of his life. He longed for the day when the great herd could be started again.

▶ What was the hope of the High Elk family?

---

6. **strain.** Lines of ancestry in a single family or breed of animal

words for everyday use

mea • ger (mē´gər) *adj.*, deficient in quantity. *The <u>meager</u> amount of food was not enough to feed five hungry children.*

The Lost Filly

Joe High Elk looked out of the window as he stood in line with the other seventh and eighth grade students. He wondered why school was being dismissed early today. The sky was just as blue as it had been an hour ago when they had returned to class after lunch. Early dismissals seldom took place in the spring. It wasn't unusual to be let out right after lunch on some days in the winter, when the prairies on the Indian reservation were often swept by blizzards, but not this late in May. The students speculated noisily among themselves.

Mr. Gray Bear rapped on his desk to get his pupils' attention again. "We've had a phone call from the police that a tornado was sighted over by Lodge Pole Ridge. But," he quickly added to reassure those whose homes were in that area, "it did not touch down. We've had the radio on and there is a severe weather watch[1] until five o'clock this evening. The buses will be here shortly, and I suggest that those of you who have over a mile to walk from your bus stop stay with friends until the storm danger is past. You students who walk or ride to school may leave if you don't have to cross the creek. If you do, then I'd like to have you stay here until the danger is over."

Mr. Gray Bear taught the seventh and eighth grades and was also principal of the consolidated elementary day school. Most of the students were bused in from the surrounding area and it would take at least an hour for many of them to get home. They began filing out of the room but Joe stopped at Mr. Gray Bear's desk.

◄ Why are students being dismissed early?

◄ What advice does Mr. Gray Bear give his students?

---

1. **severe weather watch.** Notification from the weather bureau letting citizens know that a severe storm may develop in their area

words for everyday use
spec • u • late (speˊkyə lāt) v., meditate or ponder on a subject. *Because of the storm last night, we speculate that our opponent's soccer field may be too wet to play on.*

con • sol • i • date (kən säˊ lə dāt) v., join together in one whole. *Our school district decided to consolidate two middle schools into one school.*

"Mr. Gray Bear," Joe said. "I think Marie and I had better go on home. We have to go over the creek, but the place where we cross is practically dry."

Mr. Gray Bear put his hand on Joe's shoulder and guided the boy out of the room as they talked.

"It may be dry now, Joe, but if we get a hard rain you know how bad a flash flood can be."

"Yes, I know," answered Joe. "But our filly is fast and I'd like to get home before the storm strikes. Some of our <u>stock</u> is out and Grandma is home alone. She won't be able to round them up."

"Well, it's against my better judgment to let you go, but if you move right along you should be able to make it in time. Go ahead." Mr. Gray Bear understood the tall eighth grader's concern. Indian children often assumed adult responsibility at an early age.

Joe hurried outside to the back of the school where his horse, Star, was tethered. The horizon around was still clear blue. There was no sign of a storm cloud and he felt better. 'We'll make it home okay,' he thought, for he had stretched the truth just a little when he told Mr. Gray Bear that the stock was out. There was only the old mare, who was due to foal[2] soon, and he wanted to make sure she was safe.

Maybe he was being reckless not staying safely at school especially since his little sister, Marie, would be riding double with him. But that unborn foal meant a lot to him.

Joe caught the filly and <u>bridled</u> her. She was nervous and danced away as he tried to mount her.

"Okay, girl, okay," he said soothingly. "I know the storm is coming. It's all right, Star, we'll make it home and see how your mama's doing." He calmed her, mounted and rode around to the front of the school where Marie was waiting.

▶ *Why is Joe in a hurry to get home?*

---

2. **to foal.** Give birth to a foal, a baby horse

words for everyday use

stock (stäk´) *n.*, all of the animals kept or raised on a farm; livestock. *The farmer rounded up his <u>stock</u> before the blizzard began.*

bridle (brī´dəl) *v.*, put on the headgear with which a horse is governed and which carries a bit and reins. *Sanja knew she must <u>bridle</u> her horse if she wanted to control it at the fair.*

"My teacher says we should stay here, Joe," she said, her black eyes sparkling with the fear and excitement she felt.

"We'll make it home in time, Marie. But we'll have to hurry. Come on."

Joe made a step of his foot and extended his hand to his ten-year-old sister. She was a tiny little girl and as Joe swung her up behind him her short legs stuck almost straight out on either side.

He turned the filly and urged her into a trot, and Marie tightened her arms around him to keep from bouncing off. They rode bareback[3] because their father saved the family's only saddle for special occasions. He also felt that without a saddle there was less danger of the children being injured if they ever fell from the horse.

◀ How do Joe and his sister get home? Why don't Joe and Marie use a saddle?

As they rode away from the shelter of the trees and buildings of the school and on to the open prairie, they saw the dark formation of <u>thunderheads</u> rising as high as the ridge in the west. Jagged streaks of lightning flashed continuously and they heard the thunder's rumble as the storm approached.

"Oh, Joe, I'm scared," Marie cried.

"We'll make it. Besides, you've been in storms before."

"I know," wailed his sister, "but not without Mom and Dad."

"Well, just hang on. I'm going to turn Star loose and you know how she likes to go!" Joe kicked Star into a gallop.

The filly, even with the combined weight of the two children, stretched out low to the ground. Marie's long braids flew behind her and the wind whistled in their ears as the horse sped over the level plain.

---

3. **bareback.** Without a saddle

words for everyday use   **thun • der • head** (thən´dər hed) *n.,* rounded mass of cumulus clouds often appearing before a thunderstorm. *My dad wondered if the approaching <u>thunderhead</u> would bring enough rain to fill the water bucket in the back yard.*

Almost at the creek, Joe reined Star in to check her before they went down the bank. But the filly knew she was going home and fought the bit.

"Hold on, Marie," Joe yelled. "She's not going to slow down!"

The sure-footed horse leapt down the narrow path to the creek with Joe and Marie lying low on her back to keep from being swiped off by the overhanging branches. Down they rode, splashed over the shallow stream, and started up the other side. The thunder cracked loudly, frightening the excited horse. She jumped, slipped in the mud and fell.

Joe, with Marie still tightly hanging on to his waist, threw himself clear of the falling horse. They landed, heavily, in a sumac[4] bush just as the first fat drops of rain fell.

Joe jumped up and pulled Marie with him. "Are you hurt?" he asked.

"Yes," the little girl cried, "I'm bleeding!"

Blood was running down her arm and she was frightened at the sight of it.

"Here," Joe said, "wrap my handkerchief around your arm. It's only a scratch from the bush. It'll be okay. I've got to see how Star is."

The horse had scrambled to her feet and was calmly nibbling at the grass on the side of the path. Joe whistled to her and was horrified to see her limping as she came to him. The filly was favoring her right hind leg.

"Poor girl," Joe said, petting her and feeling for other injuries. Finding none, he took the horse's reins in one hand, Marie's hand in his other, and started up the bank.

"We have to get away from the creek, Marie," he yelled over the noise of the wind which had risen and was howling through the trees. "There may be a flash flood after it starts to rain."

He pulled the horse and the little girl after him and knew that they had to find shelter soon. The wind whipped the trees, and dry branches snapped and flew around them. There were blinding flashes of

▶ What scares Star? How do Star and Marie get hurt?

---

4. **sumac.** Tree in the cashew family whose leaves turn a brilliant red in the fall

lightning followed by the loud crash of thunder. Marie stumbled and fell.

"Don't cry," Joe begged his sister as he helped her to her feet. "I'll let Star loose and carry you."

Quickly he slipped the bridle over the filly's head, wrapped and tied the reins around his waist and picked up the little girl.

"Where are we going, Joe?" asked Marie, clasping her arms tightly around his neck.

"To Grandpa's cave," he gasped. "Don't hang on so tight. You're choking me!"

◀ Where do Joe and Marie take shelter?

Joe followed the steep path up the bank and paused to rest where the faintly <u>discernible</u> trail started to parallel the creek.

"You're too heavy, Marie," he panted. "If you can walk, we'll make better time. The rest of the way is level now."

The trail was covered with dead branches and leaves, but Joe knew the path and the cave well, for he often came to this place. He had been strangely drawn to the cave ever since he had been old enough to understand that it was here that the High Elk herd had its start. Even in the driving storm Joe easily found the cave's entrance, though it was well concealed by trees. He led Marie into the dry, leaf-carpeted cave and turned to urge Star, who had followed on the path, to enter.

The filly stood, <u>peering</u> curiously through the branches, but she ignored Joe's urging.

"Come on, Star," he said, trying to grab her mane, "get in out of the rain."

The rain had started in great blasting sheets and Joe heard the roar of the water in the creek, which indicated a flash flood.

The horse slipped from his grasp and trotted back along the path, heading home to the safety of her stall. Joe, unmindful of the rain, ran after her.

---

words for everyday use

dis • cern (di sern´) v., recognize or identify as separate and distinct. *When we got close enough to the sign, I could* <u>discern</u> *that we should take the next exit.* **discernible**, *adj.*

peer (pir´) v., look narrowly or curiously. *It is impolite to* <u>peer</u> *over someone's shoulder to read whatever the person is reading.*

"Star!" he called. "Come back!" As he yelled, the frightened horse jumped as if <u>shying</u> at something and lost her footing on the wet path.

The bank crumpled beneath her and the filly slid into the rising waters of the creek. Now thoroughly bewildered, she splashed her way into the deeper channel and was swept downstream. Joe, helpless, saw her fighting the current of the flood. She broke free of the swiftly flowing waters and swam close to the far side, found her footing and scrambled out onto the bank. Joe gave a shout of relief at Star's safety, but then groaned in despair as she disappeared into the trees on the other side.

▶ *What happens to Star?*

words
for
everyday
use

shy (shī´) *v.*, jump back or to the side with fright or alarm. *The boy wanted to <u>shy</u> away from the snake.*

High Elk's Cave

WET AND COLD, Joe sat hunched on his heels, hugging his knees and staring out of the mouth of the cave. The rain was still falling, but he could tell from the way the trees stood, quietly accepting the water, that the wind had died. The storm was almost over.

"Star is gone, Star is gone." Over and over he said the sad words to himself. How could the herd begin again when part of its hope was wandering, lost along the creek? Who knew how far the horse would go in her fright? And with her injured leg she would be easy prey for wolves or wildcats, predators willing enough to feed on a filly. Full of <u>remorse</u> and despair Joe sat ignoring Marie's attempt to cheer him up.

◀ Why is Joe worried about Star?

"Don't feel bad, Joe. You couldn't help it if that dumb Star wouldn't come into the cave. She's so dumb she didn't even know enough to slow down for the slippery trail. Don't feel bad. Even if we had stayed at school. . . ." Her voice faded away as she realized that these were not cheering words.

"Yeah!" Joe cried, jumping to his feet. "We should have stayed at school! I was the dumb one thinking I could get us home before the storm struck!" He grabbed up a branch lying on the floor and beat it against the wall of the cave crying, "Dumb! Dumb! Dumb!"

◀ Why is Joe angry at himself?

In his anger at himself Joe used all of his strength to swing the branch against the side of the cave. He swung, releasing his sorrow and fury while dirt and debris, <u>gouged</u> out of the wall, flew around him.

"Joe! Joe! Stop!" screamed Marie, dodging the wildly striking branch to grab his arm. She was frightened at his fury.

"Don't! Please, Joe! Stop!"

His anger spent, Joe gave one last heave of the branch and let it fall against the wall and to the floor.

---

words for everyday use

re • morse (ri mors´) n., gnawing distress arising from a sense of guilt for past wrongs. *The young softball player felt* *remorse* *when his ball accidentally broke the neighbor's window.*

gouge (gauj´) v., scoop out with or as if with a gouge. *The child playing on the wooden seesaw had to* *gouge* *a splinter out of his finger.*

He stood, exhausted, arms hanging limply, staring, unseeing, at the wall.

He had struck repeatedly at the same spot and his wild, uncontrolled effort had dug a deep narrow hole in the wall. Looking at it he saw what he had done and was sad that in his anger he had <u>desecrated</u> the High Elk cave, which was a sacred place to him.

▶ What does Joe realize he has done?

He <u>futilely</u> tried to erase the deep depression. As his hand smoothed the raw edges of the wound he felt a soft, crumbly substance which was not dirt. Looking closely, he cautiously explored the gap he had made.

"What is it, Joe?" asked Marie. "What have you found?"

"I don't know." His hands were quickly digging away at the earth, heedless of the further damage he was doing. "There is some object—leather I think—buried here."

He took the pocket knife he always carried and began to carefully carve around the bulky shape his hands had uncovered.

▶ What does Joe find?

"See, Marie," he said. "There seems to be an old piece of leather wrapped around something."

Joe was excited now. As he dug he could see a rawhide bundle, old and rotten, that had been painstakingly tied with leather thongs.[1]

Carefully, Joe freed it from its covering of dirt. Scraps of leather flaked off as he gently placed the bundle on the floor of the cave.

"What is it, Joe?" Marie asked. "Aren't you going to open it?"

"No," he answered. "It is too dark in here to see what it is. I need something to wrap it in so that it won't fall apart."

"Here," offered Marie, "use my sweater."

"No, I'll use my shirt. Your sweater will get all dirty."

---

1. **thongs.** Narrow strips of material used to tie things together

words for everyday use

des • e • crate (de´si krāt) v., violate the sanctity of. *The town wondered who would* <u>desecrate</u> *a cemetery by overturning the gravestones.*

fu • tile (fyü´təl) adj., completely ineffective. *The sailor made a* <u>futile</u> *effort to set his boat free, but the knot was too tight.* **futilely,** adv.

"But your shirt is soaked. It'll get the whatever-it-is all wet," Marie said, placing her sweater on the floor of the cave.

"Well, I guess you're right, but I hope Mom doesn't get mad when she sees that your new sweater is dirty."

Gently and carefully, he moved the rawhide bundle and wrapped the sweater around it.

◀ How does Joe protect the treasure?

"This must be something that Grandpa buried here," Joe said, lifting the bundle into his arms.

"Grandpa?" queried Marie. "He never said anything about it."

"Not that grandpa," corrected Joe. "I mean our great-grandfather High Elk."

◀ Who might have buried the treasure?

"Wow!" said Marie. "You mean that thing has been here since the time of our great-grandfather? It really must be old."

"It is," answered Joe. "Don't you know that High Elk and his family lived here for a while?"

"Here?" said Marie, looking around at the dark, musty cave. "I thought he just kept his horses here."

"He did, but he lived in the same place so that he could always guard the horses."

"Oh, that must have been terrible!" exclaimed Marie. "I wouldn't like it at all."

Joe smiled. "You're spoiled. I bet you don't even remember when we lived in the old house without running water and electricity. Come on, we'd better head home. Grandma's probably worried about us."

The rain had stopped, but the water still dripped heavily from the trees.

"We'd better take our shoes off, Joe," Marie said, sitting down to remove hers. "They are the only ones we have and the mud will ruin them."

"Yeah," Joe agreed, admiring his little sister's practicalness, "I never thought of that."

They made a strange procession as they emerged from the cave. Joe, the reins wrapped around his waist with the bridle dangling and bumping against

---

words for everyday use

mus • ty (məs′tē) adj., smelling of damp and decay. *When we opened the cabin in the spring, it had a musty odor.*

his thigh, walked barefooted. His jeans were rolled up, and he shivered as the water dripped on his already wet shirt. In his arms he carried, like a swaddled baby,[2] the rawhide bundle carefully sheltered in Marie's sweater.

Marie followed lugging her shoes and his boots. Her long black hair, which had become unbraided, fell in tangled strands over his shoulders. She stepped carefully and distastefully along the wet, muddy path, trying to avoid soiling the full, gathered skirt of her dress.

"Careful now, Marie."

They had come to the place where the bank had crumbled under Star. The path had about a two-foot gap where the earth had fallen.

"Here, you'd better take my hand."

"I can't, Joe. My hands are full."

"Okay, I'll go first and then you hand me the shoes."

Joe's long legs easily stepped over the break. He laid the bundle down and then the shoes Marie handed him. He stretched out his hands to her and she trustingly took them. The little girl closed her eyes as she stepped across, not wanting to see the swirling, muddy, flood-filled creek below.

▶ How do Joe and Marie get home?

Safely on the firm path, the children picked up their bundles and walked up the bank, out of the trees and onto the open prairie.

They saw their house silhouetted against the gray bank of clouds which was streaked with the pink, white and blue rays of the setting sun. Far to the left, the Lodge Pole Ridge stood like a dark wall casting its shadow for miles before it.

As they followed the trail, made by generations of horses going to water at the creek, they saw the lights come on in the house, and then the bright yard light <u>illuminated</u> the old horse shed and the path before them.

---

2. **swaddled baby.** Infant strapped in strips of cloth to hold its arms and legs still

---

words for everyday use   il • lu • mi • nate (i lü´mə nāt) v., brighten with light. *We had to <u>illuminate</u> the basement with a candle when the electricity went off.*

Respond to the Selection

What do you think of the way Joe handled the weather emergency? Have you ever been caught in a big thunderstorm or snowstorm? Compare your storm experience and how you reacted to it to Joe's experience and how he reacted to it.

Investigate, Inquire, and Imagine

Recall: GATHERING FACTS

1a. How did High Elk start his horse herd? What were his horses like? Why did his herd decrease in the 1920s and 1930s?

2a. What is Joe's reason for wanting to go home when school is dismissed early?

3a. What lines in the novel show that Joe is worried about Marie and Star? Where does he decide to take them for shelter? What happens to Marie and Star?

Interpret: FINDING MEANING

→ 1b. How can High Elk's herd be enlarged again? Who will be able to increase the herd?

→ 2b. Why is Joe afraid to tell Mr. Gray Bear the reason he needs to get right home?

→ 3b. Examine Joe's behavior in the cave. Why is he so mad at himself? What does Joe do or say that illustrates how he feels?

Analyze: TAKING THINGS APART

4a. Explain the High Elk family's dreams for their land. When did their dreams begin? How have their plans been changed by outside events? Is love for the land and the horses enough? What else do they need? Compare and contrast Joe and old High Elk. How are their actions and thoughts similar? How are their actions and thoughts different?

Synthesize: BRINGING THINGS TOGETHER

→ 4b. Predict how Joe might preserve the family traditions begun by his great-grandfather High Elk. Who or what might help him?

Evaluate: MAKING JUDGMENTS

5a. Is hitting the wall of the cave a bad thing? Why, or why not?

Extend: CONNECTING IDEAS

→ 5b. What usually happens when people lose their tempers? Did that happen with Joe? Is it ever all right to lose your temper like Joe did? Why, or why not?

Understanding Literature

DIALOGUE. **Dialogue** is conversation involving two or more people or characters. Look at the dialogue in the chapter titled "High Elk's Cave." Read the chapter aloud, expressing the characters' feelings in your voice. In what way does the dialogue reveal how Marie and Joe feel about each other?

POINT OF VIEW. **Point of view** is the vantage point from which a story is told. If a story is told from the **first-person point of view,** the narrator uses the pronouns *I* and *we* and is a part of or a witness to the action. When a story is told from a **third-person point of view,** the narrator is outside the action; uses words such as *he, she, it,* and *they;* and avoids the use of *I* and *we.* From what point of view is *High Elk's Treasure* told? How do you know this? How would the story seem different if it were told from a different point of view?

PROTAGONIST. A **protagonist** is the main character in a story. The protagonist faces a struggle or conflict. Who is the protagonist in *High Elk's Treasure?* What struggle does the protagonist face in the first three chapters?

SETTING. The **setting** of a literary work is the time and place in which it happens. Writers create settings in many different ways. In fiction, setting is most often revealed by means of descriptions of landscape, scenery, buildings, clothing, the weather, and the season. It can also be revealed by how characters talk and behave. What is the setting for *High Elk's Treasure?* What descriptions in the story tell you where and what time of year the story takes place? List things that the characters say and do that reveal more about the setting for the story.

One Hundred Years

"UNCI,"[1] MARIE CALLED to her grandmother as she ran into the house.

"Takoza."[2] Joe heard his grandmother's answer as he hurried, even though wet and cold, to the old shed to check on the mare. He knew Grandma would hear Marie's story of their wet adventure and he was not ready to face the scolding he knew she would give him. Grandma High Elk could understand English and spoke it when she had to; but to her grandchildren she spoke only *Lakota*[3] and insisted that they speak it to her, so that they would know the Sioux tongue.

A soft nicker of greeting came from the shed as Joe neared it. The mare was there, safe from the storm. Joe was so relieved to find her unharmed that he put his arms around her neck and let the tears come. Quietly he sobbed into the mare's mane and she, puzzled by his strange behavior, nuzzled him gently with her lips.

"Śungwiye,"[4] he said her name quietly, slurring the guttural "g" of the word so that it was a gentle croon. "Śungwiye, will you still be my friend and give us our stallion? Oh, Śungwiye, I have been foolish. Your filly is lost."

Controlling his anguish, he did the evening chores for the mare. Her watering <u>trough</u>, which he usually filled, was overflowing with fresh rain water. He fed her the handful of oats which was her ration and filled the <u>manger</u> with hay. He stood back and watched with satisfaction as she ate. The colt was not yet ready to be born and the mare was healthy in her expectant state.

◀ What does Joe find out about the mare when he arrives home?

---

1. *Unci.* Grandmother
2. *Takoza.* Grandchild
3. *Lakota.* Means "friendly people" and is what Sioux Indians who speak Lakota call themselves
4. *Śungwiye.* Mare

words for everyday use
trough (tròf) *n.,* long, shallow, often V-shaped receptacle for the drinking water or feed of domestic animals. *On a hot day, cows gather around the watering trough.*

manger (mān´ jər) *n.,* trough or open box in a stable designed to hold feed or fodder for livestock. *The farmer put oats in the manger for his horses.*

Joe heard the motor of his parents' car as it turned off the highway. He listened to the sound of its labor as it struggled through the wet, greasy gumbo[5] of the ungraveled road. He hoped the car would not get stuck. His father would be angry enough at the loss of Star without adding the <u>aggravation</u> of a bogged-down automobile.

▶ Where do Joe and his family live?

The High Elks' home was two miles from the main paved highway that crossed the reservation. The family could have had their new, government-built house erected on a lot in the agency town where both William and his wife, Marlene, worked. Then Joe and Marie could have walked to the agency school instead of having to ride double on the filly in the varying climate of the plains. But Grandma had refused to move to town. She said she would rather stay alone in the old log shanty[6] that the first High Elk had built, where she had come as a bride and where her husband had died. William did not insist that his mother move to town, even though he and his wife would have an hour's drive to work. Also, in the back of his mind he was probably fearful that if he left the land, his dream of the High Elk horses would never be realized.

So the house was built next to the spot where the old home had stood for almost eighty-five years. Joe was glad. He loved the High Elk range bordered by the creek, the highway, and the Lodge Pole Ridge. He knew every foot of it and realized that it was unusual to find prairie ground untouched by a plow. Often, in the summer, William brought white men, <u>historians</u> from the state university, to view the grounds. They searched for Indian relics and listened attentively to William's proud recitation of his family's history. Joe

▶ Why do historians visit the High Elk lands?

---

5. **gumbo.** Fine silty soil, common in the southern and western states, that forms an unusually sticky mud when wet
6. **shanty.** Roughly built cabin

---

words for everyday use

ag • gra • va • tion (a grə vā´shən) n., act or circumstance that intensifies or makes worse. *Getting catsup on a white shirt is a big aggravation.*

his • to • ri • an (hi stōr´ē ən) n., student or writer of history. *Stephen Ambrose is a historian who has written several books about World War II.*

learned early to share his father's pride in their homestead and wanted above all to make the land a working ranch with cattle and, of course, the horses.

Joe saw the car skid and slide in the clay-like gumbo and come to a stop. His parents got out and walked toward the house.

"Dad," he called to his father. "Dad, can I talk to you before you go in?"

William, carrying a bag of groceries in his arms, hesitated at his son's call.

Joe's mother, hearing the urgency in the boy's voice, said, "Here, Will, I'll take the groceries and start supper while you talk with Joe."

Unhappily, Joe watched his father's approach. How could he tell him what had happened? The boy's throat tightened. He was not afraid of his father, with whom he had always shared his every thought, but now Joe knew that what he had foolishly caused to happen would hurt his father, and he dreaded that more than a beating.

"Hi, Joe," greeted William, and then, seeing the empty stall beside Śungwiye, asked, "Where's Star?"

"She's lost, Dad," Joe said, miserably turning to hide his face against the high gate of the corral.

◀ What does Joe tell his father?

"Lost? What do you mean?" William demanded.

Quickly, Joe told of the early dismissal from school because of the storm warning and how he decided that he could get home before the storm struck; the wild ride over the creek, Star's fall and the injury to her leg; how he and Marie took shelter in the cave; and finally, the filly's plunge into the flooded creek and her disappearance on the opposite bank.

William was silent for a long minute before he said, "I know you realize the danger that Star is in, wandering the prairie. She's not even on familiar range. From your description of where she went into the trees, she must be on the wildlife preserve. We'll need permission to go in and hunt for her. Star may

◀ What is William's plan for finding Star?

words for everyday use	home • stead (hōm´sted) *n.,* home and adjoining land occupied by a family. *The Olson's homestead was ten miles from the nearest town.*	cor • ral (kə ral´) *n.,* pen or enclosure for confining or capturing livestock. *The farmer put his horses in the corral near the barn.*

be hard to find if she joins the protected herd of wild horses, or if the <u>predators</u> frighten her into running off to the other end of the preserve."

"I know," Joe said miserably.

"I can't scold you, Joe. You should have known you needn't have worried about a wise old range mare like Śungwiye. She'd head for shelter when she first sensed the storm, long before a man would."

"All I could think about was the foal."

▶ When will they look for Star?

William nodded understandingly. "Well," he said, "there's nothing we can do tonight. When I get to work tomorrow I'll call the ranger on the preserve and ask him to be on the lookout for Star and get permission to hunt for her. We'll have to wait until Saturday to borrow horses and organize a search."

"That's two days away!" Joe cried. "Anything could happen to her in that time!"

"I know," William said, "but we can't help it. Come on, let's go eat supper."

▶ What does Joe show to his father?

"Wait," Joe said, remembering the bundle he had left in the shed. "Here, Dad, I forgot to tell you about this." He handed the sweater-wrapped package to his father and told how he had discovered it in the cave.

"Well, let's go take a look at what old High Elk hid away," said William, leading the way to the house.

Inside, Marie, who had bathed and put on clean jeans, was setting the table. Grandma was peeling potatoes and when she saw Joe she immediately started to scold.

"Has my grandson told you of his foolishness?" she said in Lakota. "He took the little girl and the filly and exposed them to the dangers of the storm. The horse is lost. *Oh hinh,*"[7] she wailed. "The pony will be eaten by the wild dogs. We should have sold her to the white man who wanted her when she was born!"

---

7. *Oh hinh.* Exclamation of shock, surprise, or fear. Similar to "Oh dear" in English

---

words for everyday use

pred • a • tor (preˊdə tər) *n.*, one that preys, destroys, or devours. *The farmer believed that a <u>predator</u> was killing the sheep in his flock.*

"Ina,"[8] William replied in Lakota. "The boy has told of his foolishness. Do not scold, he has sorrow for what has happened."

"And he should," Grandma continued, ignoring her son. "My granddaughter comes home with mud on her good school dress and see," she pointed to Joe's muddy jeans, "his good pants are ruined also. They will have to wear rags to school tomorrow, for the clothes cannot be washed and dried until the morning."

"The mud will wash out," Joe's mother said, coming into the kitchen. She had changed her white uniform to slacks and an old blouse.

"The boy was at least wise enough to take shelter so that he and Marie were safe from the storm. They also removed their shoes before walking in the mud."

Grandma disgustedly turned her back to the family. She thought her daughter-in-law was too <u>lenient</u> with the children.

◄ How does Grandma think Joe's parents treat their children?

"But, Joe," asked his mother, "where is Marie's sweater?"

"Here, Marlene," said William. "Move the dishes over for a while, Marie, so that we can see what old High Elk's treasure is."

Marie had told Marlene and Grandma about Joe's finding the leather-wrapped bundle and they came closer to see, but Grandma hung back a little.

"Téhinda,"[9] forbidden," the old woman said. She still believed many of the old superstitions. "Careful," she warned, "there may be a *wanaǧi,*[10] ghost, in it." But she moved a little nearer.

◄ How does Grandma react to the bundle?

"Do you know of this?" William asked his mother as he began to remove Marie's sweater.

Hands to her face, ready to shut out the sight of a ghost if one appeared, Grandma nodded. "My

---

8. *Ina.* Mother
9. *Téhinda.* Forbidden, taboo
10. *wanaǧi.* Ghost

---

words for everyday use

le • ni • ent (lē´ nē ənt) *adj.,* exerting a soothing or easing influence. *The <u>lenient</u> judge did not sentence the thief to jail.*

▶ How long must the bundle be undisturbed?

husband's grandfather told of how he had hidden a story thing in the cave. He warned of not disturbing it until a hundred years had passed."

"A hundred years," mused her son. "Why it must be nearly that now. Did he say the year he had hidden it?"

"No, he had no use for the year's number. It must have been after he moved into the cave."

"Let's see. We're pretty sure that he came to the reservation about 1876, for didn't he tell that it was the time of the <u>barren</u> autumn after the Little Big Horn?"[11]

"Yes," said Grandma, lowering her eyes, "he knew of that battle."

"He didn't fight Custer, did he, Grandma?" excitedly asked Joe.

Grandma covered her mouth with her hands, her eyes became blank and she mumbled, "We must not speak for a hundred years."

William looked at his mother in surprise. His mind was busy with speculations about what was in the package he was unwrapping, but he suddenly comprehended what his mother had said. He took his hands from the bundle which, free of the sweater, lay in what only seemed to be a rotten roll of rawhide. He gazed into his mother's eyes as if trying to force her to say more, but she looked away and shook her head.

Joe sensed the tension between them. "What is it? What's the matter?" he cried.

William still stood, quietly staring at his mother, then he looked at Joe as he decided what to do.

"Years ago," he explained, "almost one hundred years ago, a large gathering of the Sioux and Cheyenne

---

11. **Little Big Horn.** Village in South Dakota where Indians defeated federal troops led by Lt. Col. George Custer on June 25, 1876, leaving no white survivors

words for everyday use

bar • ren (bar´ən) adj., producing little or no vegetation. The land was <u>barren</u> after fire destroyed the forest.

defeated General Custer at the battle of the Little Big Horn."

"I know that," Joe said, wanting to forestall a history lesson and get back to whatever was wrapped in the <u>rawhide</u>.

William held up his hand to signify patience. "The soldiers who came to punish the Indians after the battle wanted very much to know who killed Custer. The warriors, who were in the battle and who knew which brave killed the general, vowed not to speak of it again for a hundred years."

◄ What did soldiers want to know about the battle?

Joe was awed. "Do you think it was Grandpa?"

"*Hinh, hinh,*" wailed Grandma. "Do not say such a thing. We will be punished!"

"Do not worry, *Ina,*" William comforted. "Whatever High Elk hid in here," he <u>reverently</u> put his hand on the bundle, "will not bring punishment on us. Those bad days are gone. It may," he went on, thinking aloud, "bring us good instead."

"Aren't you going to open it now, Dad?" Joe asked hopefully, already sensing that his father was holding back for some reason.

"Not yet. I think it is important that when we do open it, we do so in the presence of someone whose word will not be doubted."

"What do you mean?" Joe asked.

"Too often in the past our people have lost valuable tribal treasures. Whatever is in here," William said, placing his hand on the bundle, "may be valuable historically, as well as being worth money. We don't want to lose it."

"I don't understand," said Joe.

"You must remember that when the Indians were first confined to reservations they were at the mercy of the soldiers. The government wanted to wipe out the people's old way of life, and as the bands came to the reservation all of their possessions, which they valued as a free people, were taken from them. Not

---

words for everyday use

raw • hide (rò´ hīd) *n.*, untanned cattle skin. *The dog chewed on a piece of <u>rawhide</u> we bought at the pet store.*

reverent (rev´rənt) *adj.*, expressing or characterizing honor or respect. *We had a <u>reverent</u> discussion about Sherenne's grandmother.* **reverently,** *adv.*

▶ Why did Indians lie about their belongings?

only weapons, but pipes, medicine bags, *parfleches*,[12] ceremonial robes—anything that would be a reminder of their past culture—were put in a pile and burned. The Indians became sly and lied about their belongings and hid them, as High Elk probably hid this."

"That is true," said Grandma. "If a person saved something of the past it was taken from him. But not everything was burned. There were white people who took many things for their own."

William nodded his head in agreement. "Yes, they did," he went on. "And the people caught on to the white man's desire to own old things, and because they were a poor, starving people, they began to sell what little they had left. Some also learned that an article was worth more if it were thought to be very old, or if it had belonged to some famous Indian, like Crazy Horse. So some began to make things and claim that what they made had belonged to a great-grandfather, or to a well-known chief. This happened often enough to cause white people to be distrustful of any new discovery until it was checked by an expert."

"Gee," said Joe, "we'll have to be sure that everyone believes what I found is the real thing."

"That's right," William answered. "But today there are false white men who pose as experts and take a treasure from an innocent Indian, promising to prove its history. They are thieves, because they never return the article. So when we open the bundle we must do so in the presence of someone who knows about historical items, but we must make sure that he is also an honest man."

"What are you going to do?" asked Joe.

▶ Where is William going to take information about the bundle?

"Tomorrow I'll go to the tribal office and tell the council of your discovery. They'll want to know what is in the bundle and they should know an expert to contact to be here when we open it.

"But first," William continued, going to an old trunk where the family kept some things that had belonged to High Elk, "we will wrap it in High Elk's

---

12. *parfleches.* Cases made of rawhide with the hair removed

buffalo robe." He took out an old tanned hide which showed much wear, but was still intact.

"We will give it to Grandma to keep and guard," he said, handing the bundle to his mother, "for she is always at home to see that it is safe."

The old woman held it in her arms, still fearful of the *wanaǧi*. Then she carried it to her room.

◄ *Who protects the bundle?*

Wild Horse Catchers!

As HE WAS eating breakfast the next morning Joe worked out a plan to drop Marie at school and then to go on to the wildlife preserve and search for Star, even though he would have to do it on foot because he couldn't risk riding the pregnant Šungwiye. But his father <u>forestalled</u> any such notion.

"We'll give you a ride to school today, Joe," William said.

"You don't have to do that," protested Joe. "We can walk. The water in the creek must be low enough to cross. Besides, you might be late for work."

▶ Why won't Joe's mother let him look for Star right away?

"No, Joe," his mother said, "the creek and the path will be too muddy and you and Marie will be all dirty by the time you get to school."

"Don't worry about us, Joe," William added. "I want to stop at your school anyway so I can use Mr. Gray Bear's phone to call the ranger. Otherwise, I would have to wait until noon to call from work."

They arrived at school a whole hour earlier than they usually did. William went to the principal's house to explain their early arrival. Mrs. Gray Bear insisted that the children wait in the house after their parents left.

"I'm sorry about Star, Joe," Mr. Gray Bear said. "But I'm glad you're here early. You can help me and the janitor clean up the school yard."

Broken branches and other <u>debris</u> left by the storm were strewn all over the playground and Joe kept busy until classes started. In the classroom his thoughts wandered from the subject he was supposed to be studying to worrying about Star and wondering what the bundle contained. He was glad that Mr. Gray Bear didn't call on him to answer any questions.

Finally the agonizingly slow school day ended and as Joe waited for Marie he talked with Mr. Blue

---

words for everyday use

fore • stall (fôr stôl´) v., get ahead of; prevent. *My brother tired to <u>forestall</u> my father so I would have time to clean up the mess in the kitchen.*

debris (de brē´) n., scattered remains of something broken or destroyed. *<u>Debris</u> filled the factory site after the explosion.*

Shield, the High Elks' neighbor, who had come to pick up his children.

"Say, Joe," Mr. Blue Shield said, "have you folks lost your filly?"

◀ What does Mr. Blue Shield think he has seen?

"Yes, yesterday in the storm," Joe said, unhappily.

"Well, I think I saw her this afternoon."

"Where?" eagerly asked Joe.

"Well, I'm not sure it was your horse. Does she have a lame leg?"

Joe nodded and the man went on. "I was looking for strays that got away yesterday and I rode up on top of Bald Peak to get a good view of the land; you know you can see pretty far from up there."

"Yes," Joe agreed, wishing Mr. Blue Shield would hurry and tell about Star.

"I was looking east and south over your range when I saw a horse coming out of the trees by the creek. I have some new field glasses so that I can see real good for miles. Anyway, I looked and I'll be darned if it didn't look like your filly. The critter had the same star blaze on her forehead and white stockings like your filly. She was limping pretty bad."

"She wasn't cut up or anything, was she?" Joe asked.

"No, just seemed to be favoring her right hind leg."

"Gee, thanks Mr. Blue Shield. I'm going right over to have a look in that area." He started off and then remembered that the place where Mr. Blue Shield had seen Star was about ten miles from home, and he had no horse.

"Guess I can't go," he said to Mr. Blue Shield. "Śungwiye is too close to foaling to ride."

"Well, now, maybe I can help you out," Mr. Blue Shield said. "I came over with the jeep since I was looking for strays along the way. I'll get my kids and we'll drop Marie home. Then you and I can cut across your range. I'll take you south of the Bald where I think your filly is."

◀ How does Mr. Blue Shield plan to help Joe?

"Thanks, Mr. Blue Shield. I'd sure appreciate it if you would. I hate to lose any more time looking for Star."

Joe rode up in front of the jeep with Mr. Blue Shield, while Marie and the two Blue Shield girls rode in the back. The girls, all about the same age, squealed with delight as they bounced over the rough path to the High Elks'. The creek was low, although still muddy, but the four-wheel drive vehicle had no difficulty getting through.

At the High Elks' house Joe ran to the horse shed to get a rope halter and Marie <u>reluctantly</u> got out of the jeep with instructions to tell Grandma where Joe was going.

"Can't I come, Joe?" Marie begged.

"No, I'll have to move quickly if I want to catch Star and get home before dark," Joe answered. "You stay here with Grandma."

"But they get to go," Marie said, pointing to the Blue Shield girls still in the jeep.

"They're not going to hunt for Star," said Mr. Blue Shield. "I'm going to take them home after I let Joe off."

The Blue Shields' small cattle ranch was on the west of the High Elk range. They had a new house, identical to the one Joe's family lived in, built in the western foothills of the Lodge Pole Ridge. It was a lovely home site, sheltered from the <u>prevailing</u> northwest winter winds. The only problem was that the water for cattle was in a creek on the east side. Many years ago the Blue Shields had made arrangements with the High Elks to cross the cattle over their range to water. The two families were good friends as well as neighbors and the trail between their homes, which crossed above the Bald Peak, was well traveled by horse, and in recent years by the Blue Shields' jeep.

As the jeep bumped over the open plains into the foothills of the ridge, Joe scanned the horizon with Mr. Blue Shield's field glasses, looking for Star.

"That filly of yours must be a pretty smart horse," said Mr. Blue Shield. "She must have known that if she crossed the creek she'd be on home ground.

---

words for everyday use

re • luc • tant (ri lək´tənt) *adj.*, feeling or showing aversion, hesitation, or unwillingness. *Eduardo was <u>reluctant</u> to eat the cookie when he saw that it contained nuts.* **reluctantly,** *adv.*

pre • vail (pri vāl´) *v.*, be frequent. *The winds that <u>prevail</u> in the mountains are from the west.* **prevailing,** *adj.*

Something must have frightened her or I'm sure she would have headed for home."

"Did you see which way she went?" asked Joe.

"It looked to me like she was heading toward the south ridge. She must be about ten to twelve miles from home."

"I think I'll climb up on the Bald to see if I can spot her before I start searching along the south ridge," Joe planned.

◀ Where does Joe go to look for Star?

"Good idea," agreed Mr. Blue Shield. "Why don't you use my glasses, you'll be able to see everywhere with them."

"Thanks, I will."

"You can borrow one of my horses, too, if you want," the neighbor offered.

"No, I'd better not. I'd sure hate to lose one of your horses too, Mr. Blue Shield, and besides if I see Star and she's close enough to hear my whistle, she'll come."

"Okay, but if you change your mind you can sure use one. Tell you what," Mr. Blue Shield went on, "I'll take the kids on home and then in an hour or so I'll come on back to take you home. No, no," he said as Joe started to protest, "that's okay. I still have some stray stock out and I can look for them at the same time. Besides, you'd never be able to hike the ten miles home before dark. I'll meet you at the base of the Bald."

Joe got out of the jeep on the south side of the Bald Peak where the narrow trail began its steep spiral upwards. He was grateful to Mr. Blue Shield but he was vexed with himself. "I'm a stupid jerk for not thinking about how to get home." He guessed he'd planned to ride Star, forgetting about her lame leg. "Joe, you're absolutely brainless," he said out loud to the hills.

He swiftly began the climb to the top of the peak. Its base was similar to the rest of the ridge, thickly

---

words for everyday use   vex (veks´) v., irritate or annoy by petty provocations. *I vex my parents when I don't finish my homework.*

wooded with brush and the tall, straight pines for which the ridge was named. The <u>nomadic</u> Sioux had found the lightweight but strong trees ideal supports for their skin lodges.[1] About three-quarters of the way to the summit the greenery stopped and the peak jutted out over the open prairie, providing an unhampered view.

As he climbed, Joe thought of the legends of how this one peak became so bare. One story told of two monstrous bears who waged a gigantic battle to the death, uprooting trees and tearing giant boulders out of the ground. Another tale, and Joe's favorite, was of two great stallions who fought over the right to the herd of wild horses below.

Joe always vividly imagined the fury of such a fight as he recalled the story. The old king, leader of the herd for many years, accepted the challenge of a younger male who had been previously driven from the herd. Joe could almost hear them squeal with foaming mouths, as they reared and <u>lunged</u> at each other. They beat with quick kicking forehooves and deadly slashing rear ones. The maddened animals bit and ripped until both were smeared with their mingled blood. Whirling, they charged and the force of the impact hurled both to the ground. Nothing impeded their struggle. The slender pines received the <u>brunt</u> of the crashing falls until, uprooted, they toppled. Dirt and rocks flew under the stallions' sharp, scrambling hooves. At last the aged king's strength gave way to the challenger's youthful energy and speed, but he would not run. The old one fought until after one last, desperate charge, weakened by great exertion and loss of blood, he fell and could not rise. Joe would tremble as he visualized the victor striking, with rapid hooves, the final mortal

---

1. **skin lodges.** Tents made of animal skins

blow. The new monarch turned, and stood triumphant on the rim of the <u>precipice</u>, trumpeting his victory to the herd below.

The legend was still vivid in his mind as Joe quickly climbed the narrow trail which zigzagged through the pines and onto the bare crest. On top he held the glasses to his eyes and scanned the semicircle before him.

◄ *What is the legend of Bald Peak?*

Fascinated by the sudden nearness of the cars on the highway, he slowly swept the strong lenses toward his house where he could see Śungwiye contentedly browsing in the corral. The trees along the creek, the school and the wildlife preserve all seemed within touching distance. As he shifted the glasses to the south of the creek he saw from the quickened sway of the tree tops that the mustang herd was crossing.

The lead mare, emerging on the near side, paused, surveyed the open plain and galloped on, the herd following. The scrawny, wiry horses, an occasional <u>domesticated</u> breed among them, swept through the grass into the shelter of the southern ridge. Something had frightened them into leaving the protection of the preserve.

Joe moved the glasses back to the spot where the horses had come out from the trees. Two riders came galloping out of the woods and then stopped. Instinctively Joe ducked, although the men could not see him. Stretching full length on the flat rock, he held the men in sight. They seemed to be arguing about whether to follow the herd. One pointed to the way they had come, the other to the ridge ahead. Joe quickly lowered his head as he saw one man aim a pair of glasses at the ridge.

They were horse catchers, Joe knew, hunting the wild herd illegally on the preserve. The men may have deliberately stampeded the horses onto the

---

words for everyday use

prec • i • pice (pre´sə pəs) *n.,* very steep or overhanging place. *The tough mountain climber was certain he could make it over the <u>precipice</u>.*

do • mes • ti • cate (də mes´ti kāt) *v.,* adapt an animal or plant to life in intimate association with and to the advantage of humans. *Native Americans used to <u>domesticate</u> dogs to carry their belongings.*

open range where, if the men were Indian and could hunt on reservation land, the wild mustangs would be fair game. From this distance Joe couldn't tell. Their faces, in the shadow of the wide brim of their cowboy hats, were dark, but men who lived much in the out-of-doors all had sunburned skins.

▶ What does Joe see below him?

No matter if they were Indian or white, they were daring enough to break the law and, therefore, dangerous. Joe's heart was pumping madly as he thought of his lost filly. Unbranded, she would be a prime catch for lawless men.

He cautiously raised his head, but with his naked eye could not see the men. He eased the glasses up and searched. He could not spot them. It was then that he saw Star.

The filly was quite near, partially concealed in the brush of the hillock of the lower ridge to the south. She was still, staring down toward the Bald trail. Joe raised himself until he could see down the side of the ridge and spotted the horse catchers riding up. Frantic, he knew that on the next turn they would see Star. He jumped to his feet and slipped off his shirt. Yelling at the top of his lungs like a charging wild cat, he whirled the shirt over his head. Frightened, the filly snorted and turned into the sheltering brush and pines, but the men saw Joe.

▶ What does Joe do before the men discover Star?

The Rescue

JOE DUCKED DOWN among the boulders and wondered what to do. He could hear the curses of the men as they fought to get their startled horses under control.

"There's a kid up there!" one of them yelled. "He's seen us, we'd better get him!"

Joe jumped over the rocks and dead branches, running to the more difficult path down the north side of the Bald Peak. He had often climbed this faint trail looking for agates[1] and arrowheads and he knew that men on horses could not follow him. It was almost straight down. Most of the way he slid on the seat of his pants, digging the heels of his boots into the ground to slow the painful ride. Pants torn, boots badly scuffed, and with many scratches from the whipping pine branches, he landed at the bottom of the ridge. Looking up, he could not see the men, but realized they would know from the noise of his descent which way he had gone. Fearing that one of the men would use the rifle he had on his saddle, Joe traveled through the concealing brush at the base of the peak and hurried toward the road to the Blue Shields'. He had to find Mr. Blue Shield before the horse catchers could ride down the south trail.

◀ Whom is Joe hurrying to find?

He ran up the rough road and heard the motor of the jeep as it topped the rise of the ridge. Waving his arms, Joe brought Mr. Blue Shield to a brake-slamming halt.

"There are horse catchers coming down the south trail," he panted, jumping into the jeep. "And I saw Star."

"Boy, you look like you've tangled with a wildcat," exclaimed Mr. Blue Shield.

"I had to get down the north side pretty fast," Joe explained. "Those men must know I saw them chasing the mustangs out of the preserve. I scared Star away so that they wouldn't see her, but they started after me—

---

1. **agates.** fine-grained variegated stone having its colors arranged in stripes, blended in clouds, or showing mosslike forms

so I lit out down this side. I'm afraid they'll find Star," he stopped, out of breath.

"Well, now," said Mr. Blue Shield, "we'd better get out of here." He turned the jeep around on the rough road.

"What are we going to do?" asked Joe.

▶ How do Joe and Mr. Blue Shield decide to go after Star?

"We're going to my place to get a couple of horses for us to ride so that we can get that filly before those horse catchers do. This old jeep can go about any-place, but not up the Bald. I'll send my wife and kids over to your place for your dad."

"Dad won't be home until six," said Joe.

Mr. Blue Shield checked his watch. "It's almost five thirty now, by the time my wife gets there he ought to be pulling in. Let's hope he's not late. We might need his help."

Joe pulled his shirt on over his scratched and skinned back, as they drove into the Blue Shields' yard.

"You start saddling up the horses," directed Mr. Blue Shield, "while I tell the wife."

Joe ran into the corral and caught the bay mare he knew Mr. Blue Shield always rode. By the time he had finished saddling and bridling her, Mr. Blue Shield had caught another horse.

"I'd better ride bareback, Mr. Blue Shield," Joe said, handing over the reins of the horse he'd saddled. "I'm not used to a saddle."

"Okay, Joe, jump on then. These ponies are used to bareback riders. My girls ride that way all of the time," Mr. Blue Shield said as he mounted.

Mrs. Blue Shield and the girls, their eyes round with excitement, were driving up the road as the man and boy rode out of the yard.

"We'll let them go on before us," Mr. Blue Shield said. "The sound of the jeep's motor might scare those horse catchers into being cautious."

"Gosh, I hope they haven't found Star," Joe said.

"I don't think they have yet. It'll take them a while to get down the south trail and around to the north side to see where you went."

"What will we do if we see them?" Joe asked nervously.

"That depends on what they do," answered Mr. Blue Shield.

As they rode down to the base of the Bald they saw the jeep bouncing over the range toward the High Elks'.

"We'll act like we're looking for strays," instructed Mr. Blue Shield.

◀ How will Joe and Mr. Blue Shield act when they meet the horse catchers?

They scanned the ridge as they walked the horses around to the north side. Mr. Blue Shield used his field glasses to get a better view. As they rode near the bottom of the trail, Joe saw the horse catchers.

"There they are," he said softly, "and they've got Star."

Mr. Blue Shield made no comment, but continued riding up to the men.

The horse catchers had lassoed the filly. One of the men was mounted. He was backing his horse, attempting to keep the rope <u>taut</u> around Star's neck. The other man, on foot, was vainly trying to slip a halter over the head of the struggling horse. Star's ears were flat and she was snorting and snapping at the man on the ground as she whirled closer to slash her hind hooves at the mounted horse. The men were yelling and clearly having a difficult time. They didn't hear the approach of the man and boy.

◀ What are the horse catchers doing?

"I see you found one of the strays we've been looking for," said Mr. Blue Shield calmly.

The men ceased struggling with Star. The rope hung loosely from her neck and from the mounted man's saddle. The filly lowered her head and began browsing unconcernedly.

"Whatta you mean, your stray?" the mounted man asked <u>belligerently</u>. "This ain't no tame horse, she's as wild as any mustang."

"She's mine," said Joe.

The man looked closely at Joe, recognizing him as the boy who had startled his horse. "Say, you're the kid who spooked our horses. Now what did you do that for?"

---

words for everyday use

taut (tȯt´) adj., having no give or slack. *The taut rope kept the horse from reaching the apples on the ground.*

bel • lig • er • ent (bə lij´rənt) adj., inclined to or exhibiting assertiveness, hostility, or combativeness. *A belligerent parent argued with the referee because he thought the call was unfair.* **belligerently,** adv.

"I didn't want you to get my horse," answered Joe, pointing to Star.

The man looked at Star and said, "You can't prove she's yours, she ain't branded."

Joe glared helplessly at the mean-looking white man, but before Joe could answer him Mr. Blue Shield said, "You men must be new around here, not to know a High Elk horse." He was staring at the younger man who stood nervously coiling the halter rope. As Mr. Blue Shield spoke the young man looked up and they saw that he was an Indian, not too much older than Joe.

"Are you High Elk?" the strange young Indian asked Mr. Blue Shield.

"I am," answered Joe.

"You?" The young man looked startled.

"Joe High Elk," Joe explained. "My dad is William and we own this filly."

"I still say you can't prove it," said the white man. "If she's a tame horse, how come she put up such a fight when I tried to halter her?"

"She's been ridden only by High Elks and handled only by High Elks since she was born. Maybe she doesn't like your smell!" Joe retorted, urging the horse he was riding nearer to Star, who now stood nervously watching Joe.

The white man was angry. "You're a pretty mouthy kid, ain't you?" he said, barring Joe's approach to Star. "I say the filly's wild and claim her 'cause we caught her." He motioned to the man on the ground to grab hold of the dangling rope.

"I'll prove she's mine," Joe said, dismounting. "I can walk right up to her and she'll let me mount her, even without a halter!"

"Wait!" ordered the white man to his partner. "Hang on to that rope."

But the young Indian dropped the rope. "Let the kid try," he said.

Joe walked slowly to Star. He hoped that all the excitement she'd been through wouldn't have made her wary of everyone.

"Easy, Star. Good girl," he said in a quiet, reassuring tone.

The filly stood still as he approached, ears perked forward at his voice. She gave a small nicker as his hand went to her face.

"How are you, girl?" Joe went on in the same gentle tone, all the while patting and stroking the filly's back as he eased his way to her side. She trembled as he grabbed a hand hold in her mane to swing himself up to her back, but she let him mount.

"Good girl," Joe said thankfully. He had never before mounted Star without a bridle or halter to control her. He felt lucky that she'd permitted it now. He loosened the lasso and slid it over her head. Star shook her head as the rope fell, glad to be free of its restraint.

◀ How does Joe prove that Star is his horse?

"Guess that proves it," said Mr. Blue Shield. "I think you guys better get out of here. You're on private land."

Thwarted, the white man angrily coiled the lasso to his saddle horn. "Come on," he said to his partner, and rode off.

The young Indian climbed onto his horse, which he had tied to a nearby bush. He hesitated as if to say something, changed his mind and cantered after the white man.

"Better stay out of the preserve too," warned Mr. Blue Shield.

Joe eased himself off the filly, fearful that any abrupt movement would startle her into running off again. Keeping a hand in her mane, he slipped the halter over her head and started leading her home.

As Joe and Mr. Blue Shield headed for the High Elk home, they heard the motor of the jeep and saw it speeding toward them.

"That must be your dad," said Mr. Blue Shield. "My wife's too scared to drive that fast."

"You've found Star," said William as he braked the jeep. "Where? And where are the horse catchers?"

"Hold on," said Mr. Blue Shield dismounting, "you ride home with Joe and he'll tell you all about it. I'll take the jeep to collect my family."

"Well, Joe," said the boy's father. "Seems like you have another story to tell me."

Respond to the Selection

What could be in the bundle? Do you think it will change the High Elks' lives? Why, or why not?

Investigate, Inquire, and Imagine

Recall: GATHERING FACTS

1a. In the chapter "One Hundred Years," Joe is worried about two things. What is Joe most worried about? What else is Joe worried about? How does his family react to his worries?

2a. List ways in which Mr. Blue Shield helps the High Elk family in "Wild Horse Catchers!" and "The Rescue."

3a. How does Mr. Blue Shield tell Joe to act when they meet the horse catchers? How does "the mean-looking white man" try to keep Star? How does Joe prove that Star is his horse?

Interpret: FINDING MEANING

1b. Joe almost forgets to tell his father about the bundle he finds. Why do you think he almost forgets about it?

2b. Retell the two legends of Bald Peak. Why does Joe prefer the second legend?

3b. Some of what Joe and Mr. Blue Shield say is not entirely the truth. Why do they say things that are not entirely true?

Analyze: TAKING THINGS APART

4a. Historians who have visited the High Elk ranch in the past and the horse catchers that Joe runs in to believe that the High Elks have things that are valuable. Explain which High Elk possession each group finds valuable. Why does each group believe that the High Elks' possessions are valuable? Which group is the most dangerous? Why?

Synthesize: BRINGING THINGS TOGETHER

4b. Do the High Elks have reasons to be afraid of outsiders' opinions and actions? When should the High Elks listen to the advice of other groups? What should the High Elks do about the dangerous groups?

Evaluate: MAKING JUDGMENTS

5a. Why do the High Elks decide to wait and open the bundle with a historian present? Do you think they have made the right decision? Explain.

Extend: CONNECTING IDEAS

5b. What would you have done if you had found the bundle? What things do you need to worry about when you find something valuable like that?

Understanding Literature

CONFLICT. A **conflict** is a struggle between two people or things in a literary work. This struggle can be internal or external. A struggle that takes place between a character and some outside force such as another character or nature is called an *external conflict*. A struggle that takes place within a character is called an *internal conflict*. In the beginning of *High Elk's Treasure,* Joe has an internal conflict about whether or not he should tell his teacher, Mr. Gray Bear, that he wants to get home right away to check on Śungwiye. Joe decides not to tell Mr. Gray Bear about Śungwiye; he only tells Mr. Gray Bear that his grandmother may need help and he needs to check on his stock. In the "Wild Horse Catchers!," Joe and Mr. Blue Shield both have an external conflict with the horse catchers. Describe what each of them says and does to manage the conflict with the horse catchers. Why do they deal with the conflict in this way?

ORAL TRADITION. An **oral tradition** is works, ideas, or customs of a culture, passed by word of mouth from generation to generation. What customs have been passed down by oral tradition in the High Elk family? What customs mentioned on page 21 does Grandma think are being forgotten? Are any of these customs in danger of being forgotten? What customs have been passed down in your family? What things does your family do in a special way? Does your family have stories about any objects in your house—old pictures, furniture, clothes, or other special items? Do you have special celebrations or decorations on holidays or birthdays?

LEGEND. A **legend** is a story coming down from the past, often based on important real events or characters. What stories have been passed down in the High Elk family? Why do you think these stories are important to the High Elks? What stories have been passed down in your family? What other legends have you heard?

MOTIVE. **Motive** is a reason for acting in a certain way. What motives do the following people have for looking for Star: Joe, Mr. Blue Shield, and the mean-looking white man?

Howard High Elk

THE BLUE SHIELDS stayed for supper with the High Elks at Marlene's insistence. As they ate, Joe and Mr. Blue Shield told the details of their encounter with the horse catchers.

"Did you recognize the men?" asked William.

"No," answered Mr. Blue Shield, "I never saw either of them before. But, you know, there was a young Indian with them and he reminded me of someone, but I can't think of who it could be."

▶ What does Mr. Blue Shield say about one of the horse catchers?

The two men and Joe went out to the horse shed to check on Śungwiye and Star while the women cleaned up after supper. Marie, who seldom had company, was happily playing with the Blue Shield girls.

"Looks like the filly is glad to be home," said Mr. Blue Shield as he watched Star contentedly munching hay.

William nodded. "She's lucky that her leg isn't too badly hurt." He had examined it earlier and found the injury to be only a sprain, which he had firmly bandaged to give support as it healed.

"You kids will have to walk to school for several weeks," he said to Joe.

Joe nodded. That wouldn't be so bad, as there were only a few weeks of school left.

"You can ride my horses tomorrow," kindly offered Mr. Blue Shield.

"Thanks," said William. "Leave both horses here and Joe can return them to your place after school."

"Your mare's due soon, isn't she?" asked their neighbor.

"Should be any day now," replied William. "Joe, here, has been babying her so that she ought to give a healthy foal."

▶ What does Mr. Blue Shield say about High Elk horses?

"I hope she gives you a stud colt," Mr. Blue Shield said, knowing of their dreams. "My father had one of your horses and it was the best all-around ranch horse we ever had. There should be more of them. Well," he turned toward the house, "I better round up my family. I have a few chores to do before dark."

"Thank you for your help, Albert. I'm glad we got Star back. Joe couldn't have done it alone."

"That's okay, Will," his friend answered. "You've helped me out many times in the past. Guess that's what neighbors are for."

"Thank you, Mr. Blue Shield," said Joe. "Dad's right, I couldn't have caught Star alone. When she's well I'd sure be glad to lend a hand on your ranch this summer." He wanted to do something for the man who had done so much for him.

"Say, Joe, I just might take you up on that offer. My girls don't make very good cowboys and there are times when I could use another hand."

The three girls protested at not being able to play longer, but Mrs. Blue Shield invited Marie to come to their house soon and Marlene promised that she could.

Joe and his father stood watching their neighbors ride off in their jeep. "That's a good man to have for a friend and neighbor," William said. "I'm glad you offered to help him, Joe. Now don't take any money if he offers it."

"Oh, I won't, Dad," and then remembering the bundle he said, "Did you talk to anyone about the thing I found in the cave?"

"Yes, I did," his father said. "I called the tribal chairman, Frank Iron Cloud. He agreed with me that we should have an expert on hand when we open the bundle. He suggested I call Dr. Scott—you remember, he's one of the men from the university who was out here last summer. He and Frank will drive out here tomorrow."

◄ *Who is Dr. Scott?*

"What did Dr. Scott say?" asked Joe.

"He sounded pretty excited over the phone. He was pleased that I had called him to be an 'authoritative witness,' as he put it."

"What do you think it is, Dad?"

"I don't even want to guess. It might be of value and then it could be just an old rolled-up strip of rawhide. We'll have to wait and see."

---

words for everyday use

au • thor • i • ta • tive (ə thôr´ə tā tiv) *adj.*, having or proceeding from authority; official. *We have heard from authoritative sources that the new school will open soon.*

<u>Musing</u> over the possibilities of what the bundle might contain, they started toward the house.

"Hey, what's that?" Joe said, hearing a noise. "Listen, I thought I heard a horse."

"Well, we have four of them here," his father said. "Quite a herd for a change."

"No," Joe insisted. "What I heard seemed to be coming from the creek."

They stood, straining their ears to the early evening's unbroken quiet. Suddenly they heard the neigh of a horse, closer this time, and one of the Blue Shield horses whinnied in reply.

"You're right, Joe. There's a rider coming up the path from the creek."

▶ Who rides up the path?

They waited and as the mounted figure came nearer, Joe recognized him as the young Indian he'd seen with Star. "It's one of the horse catchers!"

William walked toward the approaching horse. "What do you want?" he demanded.

The young man reined in by the corral. "Are you High Elk?" he asked.

"Yes, I am. What do you want?" Joe's father asked.

"Don't want to cause any trouble, I've had enough. . . ." The strange Indian's voice faded as he swayed in the saddle.

Quickly William was at the horse's side. "You're hurt. Here Joe, take care of his horse. I'll help him in to the house."

"But, Dad," Joe protested, "he's one of the men who tried to steal Star!"

"Never mind, Joe. This boy is hurt and we'll help him." William assisted the young man down and supported him to the house.

Puzzled as to why the young Indian would come to the High Elks' home, Joe quickly unsaddled the horse, slipped its bridle, turned it into the corral with the Blue Shield horses and ran into the house.

words
for
everyday
use

muse (myüz´) v., become absorbed in thought. *Ian had time to <u>muse</u> about which classes he should take next fall.*

42   HIGH ELK'S TREASURE

William had put the young man on the bed in the living room and was pulling the boy's soiled boots off.

"I'm okay. I can sit up, I don't want to be a bother," the stranger protested.

"But your face," said Marlene.

Joe walked closer and saw the young man's face was bruised and battered, one eye was swollen shut and dried blood covered a cut on his cheek.

The young Indian lifted a hand to his apparently painful eye, "Yeah, I bet I really look rough. Martin sort of knocked me around."

◄ Who hurt the young rider?

"Martin?" asked William. "Is that the white man you were with?"

The boy nodded. "He didn't like it much when I let you mount your horse," he said to Joe. "Then when I told him I was splitting, he really got mad." He sat up holding his head.

"Marlene," William said, "fix him something to eat. Come," he said to the boy, "let's get you cleaned up and see how badly you've been hurt. Then you can tell us about it."

Later, his face cleansed and a Band-Aid over the cut, the young man sat at the table eating hungrily.

"Now, first off," William asked, "who are you?"

"My name is Howard Anderson since my stepfather adopted me, but my real last name is Pretty Flute."

◄ Who is the young rider?

"Pretty Flute?" mused William. "There used to be a family of that name on this reservation."

The boy nodded, "Yes, my dad was born at the agency, but moved to Los Angeles after the Second World War." He paused and looked at William. "My mother's maiden name was Irene High Elk. Her father was Howard High Elk."

The family was quiet, surprised at the boy's identity. Grandma's keening wail broke the silence.

"*Oh hinh.* I know of this Irene. She once wrote a letter to my husband. Her man had died and she needed money to raise her young son. But we had bad times and had nothing to send. My husband was sad about not being able to help his niece. We always wondered what happened to her and the boy."

"Can you tell us whatever happened to your grandfather, Howard High Elk? We have never known where he went after he sold the land and horses," William explained.

"Yes, I can," Howard answered. "Grandpa told me everything about himself. He moved somewhere in Nebraska and lived there until all of his money was gone. His daughter was born there, but when she was a baby the family moved near Beulah, Wyoming. Howard worked for a rancher there. He always loved horses and in the last years of his life he regretted leaving this place. He always wanted to bring Irene here to visit, but was not sure of the welcome he would get. I don't know how my mother met my father, but it was during the war, and after it was over they moved to California.

"Grandpa got too old to work, and he was so lonely after Grandma died that he moved to live with us in California. I remember him very well because after my father died, I used to stay home with Grandpa while Mom worked. He used to talk about the famous High Elk herd and how he always wished he could see it again. He told me the story of High Elk's cave, and the stallion legend of Bald Peak."

Howard paused to take a drink of water, then continued.

"After he died my mother got married again to a white man, George Anderson. He was okay. He was good to me and we got along all right, but then he moved us to Wyoming. He had worked for the Bureau of Indian Affairs Employment Service in Los Angeles and that's where my mother met him when she went there to get help in finding a job. Well, he was tired of the city and transferred to Wyoming. I was sort of excited about moving. My step-dad said I could have a horse, which I always wanted, because of Grandpa's stories I suppose.

"At first it was fine when we moved last summer. I got my horse, learned to ride and really liked the mountains where we lived, but then school started."

Again he paused, as if wondering how to tell the rest.

"You know, I never thought much about being an Indian. I knew I was, but didn't think that made me different from anyone else. Where I went to school in L. A. there were all kinds of people: blacks, Japanese,

▶ Where did Howard's grandfather go?

whites, Chicanos[1] and a few Indians. We got along okay. But in the new school, I didn't know what I was. The white kids called me an Indian, like it was a dirty word; the Indian kids called me a white man because of my step-dad. I didn't have any friends. I got into fights and started skipping school—I hated the place! Then I was suspended. My mom cried. My step-dad got mad. They didn't know what to do with me. I knew I was a big problem, so I split."

◀ What was Howard's new school like?

"Split?" asked William, puzzled at the term.

"You know, Dad," said Joe. "He left. Ran away."

"Right," Howard continued. "I really didn't know where I was going, but I <u>bummed</u> in this direction."

"You hitchhiked?" asked Joe.

"Yes. When I got to the town north of this reservation I knew I had to come here, but wasn't sure how. I got a job at a gas station there and then met Martin, who used to hang around the place. When he found out I could ride he asked me if I wanted a job rounding up wild horses. I didn't know anything about wild horses, except for what grandpa used to tell and I thought it would be a great job and a chance to get down here. I honestly didn't know," he said to William, "that we would be hunting on a protected preserve or that I was even anyplace near the High Elk land.

"Martin had a cattle truck that we came down in with two horses in the back. He said I could have one of the horses to keep for helping him. He also said he'd pay me half the money after he sold the wild horses we caught. It sounded like a good deal. But now I know that Martin is a crook and probably wouldn't have paid me anything.

"When I found out where I was, and who you were," he said to Joe, "and that we were trying to steal a High Elk horse, I was just sick.

◀ How does Howard feel about what he has done?

---

1. **Chicanos.** Mexican Americans

words for everyday use   **bum** (bəm´) v., obtain by begging. *The out-of-work actor tried to <u>bum</u> a ride to California.*

"Man, I wanted to get away from that Martin, but I was afraid of him. He chewed me out good for letting you get the filly and I told him I was through. That's when he hit me. He knocked me down, jumped on his horse and left me by the creek. Why he didn't take my horse, I don't know."

"The horse was probably stolen," said William. "Boy, you've had quite a time. How old are you?"

"Almost eighteen. I would have graduated from high school this year if I'd stayed in school," Howard said sadly.

"I bet your mother is worried sick about you," said Marlene. "We'll have to let her know you're here."

"Yes," said William, "we'll do that tomorrow, but for now you can bed down in Joe's room. No," he said as Howard started to protest. "You're our boy, just as if you had always lived here. We Indians take care of our own."

Joe and Howard

THE DAY IN school passed even more slowly than the previous one had. The excitement of Star's rescue and of having a member of the long-lost Howard High Elk family appear and then to have this relative turn out to be one of the horse catchers was almost too much for Joe to comprehend. Most exciting of all would be this evening's visit from Frank Iron Cloud and Dr. Scott. Would they finally get to open the mysterious bundle? Joe couldn't even begin to concentrate on his studies with such things on his mind.

◄ What is on Joe's mind?

At last, he was able to pick up Marie and head for home. They were riding one of the Blue Shields' horses which was older and slower than Star. Joe couldn't even kick her into a trot and it seemed forever before they got home.

Howard was waiting by the corral as they rode into the yard. He had his horse saddled and the other Blue Shield horse ready to go.

"Hi," he greeted Joe and Marie. "I'll ride over to the Blue Shields with you, Joe, so that you won't have to walk back."

"Has Śungwiye had her baby yet?" asked Marie, running into the shed to see for herself.

"Not a baby," corrected Joe. "That's what people have. Horses have foals." He followed her into the shed.

"Well, it'll still be a baby," said Marie.

"The mare acts sort of restless," Howard said. "She's been nipping at Star and wouldn't let me touch her when I went in to water her."

◄ How is Śungwiye acting?

"She doesn't know you yet, Howard," said Marie.

The boys looked at each other and laughed, both remembering Star's aversion to strangers yesterday.

Śungwiye was now standing calmly in her stall. She nickered softly at Joe as he walked in beside her, gently running his hand over her neck. Star also gave greeting, wanting her share of attention, but the mare laid her ears back and reached her head over the stall's <u>partition</u> to nip at the filly.

"What's the matter, Śungwiye?" <u>crooned</u> Joe. "Is it getting about time for that foal to come?" The mare tossed her head as if she agreed with him.

Joe walked into Star's stall. "Come on Star, we better get you out of the maternity ward. Śungwiye doesn't want you around." He led the filly into the corral and saw that she was still favoring her bandaged leg. You'll be okay out here. We're taking the other horses home."

Grandma came to the corral as Joe led Star out of the shed.

"That is a good idea," she said, "to let the mare be alone in her stall."

"Do you think she'll be all right while we take the Blue Shield horses home?" asked Joe.

Grandma gave a little laugh. "There is nothing you can do. Śungwiye is a wise old mother, she will not need help and it will be a while before it happens."

"Well, we'll hurry back," Joe said and then it occurred to him that Grandma had been speaking English. As they rode off, leading the horse, he teased her in Lakota, "Hey, *Unci, waśicun niye un?*"[1]

"Humph," Grandma grumbled and then commanded, *"Iyopte!"*[2]

Joe rode off laughing.

"What was that all about?" asked Howard, who hadn't understood a word.

"I'm sorry, Howard," Joe said, still laughing. "I guess I'm not as polite as Grandma. She so seldom speaks English that I forget that she can. She was being considerate of you because she knew you can't understand Lakota. I had to tease her a little bit and

▶ *What language does Grandma use most?*

---

1. *Unci, waśicun niye un?* Grandmother, are you a white woman now?
2. *Iyopte!* Get going!

words for everyday use

par • ti • tion (pär ti′shən) *n.,* something that divides, such as an interior dividing wall. *A <u>partition</u> separates our living room from our dining room.*

croon (krūn′) *v.,* speak or sing in a gentle murmuring manner. *I heard my mother <u>croon</u> a lullaby to my baby sister.*

I asked her if she was a white woman now and she got disgusted with me and said to 'Get going!'"

The boys laughed. "I'd like to learn how to talk Indian," Howard said. "Why do you call the language 'Lakota' instead of Sioux?"

"It's complicated and I'm not sure I really understand why," Joe said, "but I'll try to explain.

"The Sioux have different ways of pronouncing the same word. I think it is called an accent. No," pondered Joe, "that's not right."

"Do you mean '<u>dialect</u>?'" Howard suggested.

"Yes, that's the word. Dialect. Some of the Sioux used the 'd' in their dialect and others used the 'l' so that 'Dakota' became 'Lakota' even though they were the same word. In the Lakota dialect all words with a 'd' sound are replaced by the 'l' sound. The word 'thank you,' for example, is *'pidamiye'* in Dakota. The Lakota change it to *'pilamiye.'*"

◀ How are the Dakota and Lakota dialects different?

"Wow," exclaimed Howard. "That sounds difficult. I don't think I'll ever be able to learn to speak Sioux— I mean Lakota."

"It's not hard," protested Joe. "If you are around here very long you'll have to learn. Grandma will get tired of talking English and then we'll all have to speak Lakota to her."

"I guess my family lived with white people too long, because we speak only English at home." Thinking of his home, Howard added, "I talked to my mother on the telephone this morning."

William had taken Howard into the agency with him this morning to make the call.

"What did she say?" asked Joe.

"She was glad to hear my voice and happy to know where I was. I talked to my step-dad too. I was afraid that he would be angry, but he apologized to me. He blamed himself for my running away because he'd been so mad at me before."

◀ How do Howard's parents react to hearing from Howard?

"Are they coming after you?"

---

words for everyday use

di • a • lect (dī′ ə lekt) *n.*, regional variety of a language distinguished by unique vocabulary, grammar, or pronunciation. *Many people in Texas speak with a southern <u>dialect</u>.*

"Not for two weeks. They can't get away from work until then, but your father said I could stay here and maybe help Mr. Blue Shield out. I guess your neighbor will be busy with cows calving and can use help."

"I'm glad you can stay for a while longer," Joe said happily. "I can show you all around the High Elk range. What about your horse?" he asked, referring to the animal which they thought Martin had stolen.

"Your father reported Martin to the police and also told them about the horse. They'll keep an eye out for reports of a stolen horse, but said I might as well keep her out here until they hear something. The police said the chances of finding out who the horse belonged to were slim, because Martin had a suspicious record of all kinds of illegal activities, such as <u>rustling</u>, as well as capturing wild horses. Man, am I glad I got away from him before I really got into trouble."

When the boys arrived at the neighboring ranch, Mr. Blue Shield was surprised, but pleased, at Howard's identity. "I thought you reminded me of someone," he said. "I knew your father, and you resemble him."

▶ *What does Howard offer to do?*

"I'm going to be around for the next two weeks, Mr. Blue Shield," Howard said. "I'd be willing to work for you if you can use me."

"Yes, I sure can use some help now," Mr. Blue Shield said accepting Howard's offer. "Even if my girls were old enough to lend a hand, I couldn't take them out of school. I'd be glad to pay you," he offered.

"No, sir," refused Howard. "I want to do it for nothing. Besides I'm green at ranch work and might not be as much help as you'd like."

The boys refused Mrs. Blue Shield's invitation to lunch, explaining that Śungwiye might be going into labor. They rode off in high spirits.

---

words for everyday use   rus • tle (rə´səl) v., steal cattle. *Last night, someone tried to <u>rustle</u> the farmer's steers.*

"Man, this is an uncomfortable ride," complained Joe, who was sitting in back of Howard.

"The saddle seat is more comfortable," laughed Howard. "Why do you always ride bareback?"

"We only have one saddle," Joe explained, "and we save that for special occasions because we couldn't afford a new one if that wore out. Anyway, Dad also says that it's safer riding bareback because Marie and I ride double to school. At least, there is no danger of being hung up in a <u>stirrup</u> if we ever get thrown."

◀ Why is Joe used to riding bareback?

The boys, in spite of their age difference, were enjoying each other's company. Howard listened sympathetically to Joe's story of how he'd lost Star and how angry he'd been at himself.

"I know how you felt," Howard said, thinking of his own exploits. "I guess we both have to learn to use a little common sense."

They eagerly asked and answered questions about each other. Joe wanted to know what it was like living in a big city since he'd never seen one. Howard was curious about the reservation and ranching. He listened intently when Joe spoke of his hopes for the High Elk herd.

◀ What do Joe and Howard talk about?

"Look," Howard said as the High Elk house came into view, "aren't there two cars at your place?"

"Yes," agreed Joe, peering ahead. "Mom and Dad must be home early and—oh, hurry! It must be Mr. Iron Cloud and the man from the university."

Howard kicked the horse into a <u>canter</u> as Joe told him of the mysterious bundle and how he wanted to be present when it was opened.

Riding up fast into the yard they saw that the whole family, Mr. Iron Cloud, and a tall, gray-haired white man were gathered around the horse shed.

"Śungwiye!" yelled Joe. "Has she had a colt?"

"No, not yet," answered William, emerging from the mare's stall. "But I don't think it will be long.

---

words for everyday use

stir • rup (stər´əp) *n.,* one of a pair of frames attached to a saddle for the rider's feet. *I put my foot in the <u>stirrup</u> and got on my horse.*

can • ter (kan´tər) *n.,* three-beat gait resembling but smoother and slower than the gallop. *After riding in the parade, the mounted police officer was able to let her horse <u>canter</u> through the field.*

No," he said, taking Joe's arm as the boy started into the shed, "we'll leave her alone. She knows what to do and our presence will just make her nervous. Come into the house now. We'll check on her in a little while."

"Gosh, Dad, I can't begin to sit still. Oh, man, everything happens at once!"

▶ Why are Mr. Iron Cloud and Dr. Scott at the High Elk's house?

Joe's father laughed at the boy's <u>agitation</u>, "I know, but don't you want to greet Mr. Iron Cloud and Dr. Scott who are here to open the High Elk bundle?"

"How do you do," said the tall white man. "I understand you've been having a lot of excitement around here."

"Hello, Joe. I'm glad you found your filly," greeted Mr. Iron Cloud.

Joe, remembering his manners, shook hands with the men. "Hello, Dr. Scott, Mr. Iron Cloud. I'm sure glad you're here. I guess this has been about the most exciting and worried time of my life!"

Laughing at Joe, the group moved into the house, but Joe noticed that Howard stayed behind.

"Dad, I told Howard about the High Elk thing," Joe said, wanting his new friend and relative to share the family's discovery.

William turned and called, "Come with us, Howard. This is your <u>heritage</u> too."

---

words for everyday use

ag • i • ta • tion (aj ə tā´ shən) n., emotional disturbance. *Barrett's little brother suffered extreme <u>agitation</u> when Barrett threw the ball over the fence.*

her • i • tage (her´ə tij) n., something transmitted by or acquired from a predecessor. *My great-grandmother's quilt is part of my family's <u>heritage</u>.*

The High Elk Treasure

THE GROUP QUIETLY seated themselves around the kitchen table. Grandma brought the bundle, from which she had gently taken the buffalo hide, and placed it in the center of the table. She remained standing, a little distance from them. *"Téhinda,"*[1] she murmured.

◀ Who brings the bundle to the table?

"Now, *Ina,*"[2] William said soothingly, "the hundred years are almost over and I believe old High Elk only meant to keep his secret hidden until the danger of punishment was past."

"Open it, Joe," he said, motioning to his son. "You should have the honor, since you discovered it."

"No, I can't," Joe said, shaking his head. "I'm too nervous. Dr. Scott, you open it."

William nodded at the white man to go ahead. Dr. Scott began to undo the leather thongs, but they were rotten and fell apart in his hands.

◀ Who opens the bundle?

"Was it in this condition when you found it?" he asked Joe.

"Yes. It was buried in the wall of the cave, and looked just like it does now."

Worriedly, Dr. Scott shook his head, "I hope its contents are in better condition than the outer covering. I imagine the cave is a damp place since it is so near the creek."

"No," William said. "The cave is well above the water line and dry."

The thongs off, Dr. Scott began to carefully unroll the rawhide. There were several layers of it; some peeled away easily, but in spots it tore away as if it had been glued together.

"It seems to have been partially sealed with something. It is a sticky, oily substance, I'm not sure, but it may be creosote."[3]

"It might be the tar pitch of a pine tree," guessed William. "The old Indians knew how to use it for waterproofing."

---

1. **Téhinda.** Forbidden, taboo
2. **Ina.** My mother
3. **creosote.** Yellowish to greenish brown, oily liquid obtained from coal tar and used as a wood preservative and disinfectant

"That could be," said Dr. Scott. "I'll have it chemically analyzed, but whatever it is, it seems to have protected the inner layer of the rawhide."

He removed the last of the outer covering and disclosed a bulky, <u>oblong</u>, envelope-shaped bag. "Why it's a parfleche," he said, excitement sounding in his voice.

▶ How is the bundle wrapped?

The parfleche was a heavy duty storage packet used to store dried food or personal belongings. They were made, as was this one, by folding a single wet sheet of rawhide into the desired form.

"Why, you can still see the design on it," <u>marveled</u> Marlene.

"Yes, someone, probably High Elk's wife, took great pains to paint it carefully as well as artistically," said Dr. Scott, gently lifting the parfleche to examine it. "It is in surprisingly good shape, just a little decay on the corners."

He opened it and found another leather-wrapped package inside.

"This," he said, taking the smaller bundle out, "is of tanned hide, probably elk or deer. It is very soft and smells sweet," he mused as he unrolled it. The <u>pungent</u> odor reached the group gathered around the table. Dr. Scott found the source of the spicy scent in a braided stalk of grass rolled in the leather wrapping.

"Sweet grass," he said. "Didn't the Indians use this as we use a sachet?"[4]

"Yes," answered Marlene, "we still do. We have some that Grandma braided in our storage trunk."

Dr. Scott nodded. "Now," he breathed, "we come to whatever was precious enough to merit such care."

A smaller piece of tanned hide was rolled within the outer one. Gently, with extreme care, he spread it flat on the table.

---

4. **sachet.** Small bag containing a perfumed powder

words for everyday use

ob • long (ä´bloŋ) *adj.*, deviating from a square, circular, or spherical form by elongation in one dimension. *The oblong board wouldn't fit in the car.*

mar • vel (mär´vəl) *v.*, become filled with surprise or wonder. *Neighbors marvel about the miracle.*

pun • gent (pən´jənt) *adj.*, causing a sharp or irritating sensation. *The pungent odor of the moldy orange made me gag.*

"Look, there are pictures painted on it," Joe said. "What is it?"

"This is fantastic!" The historian was amazed at the discovery. "It is a pictograph narrative."[5] He bent closer to examine it. "It must be the record of some important event, but it is too small to be of the Winter Count[6] type."

◀ What is in the bundle?

"Aren't those soldiers?" Joe asked, placing his finger on the crudely drawn figures which seemed to be scattered in one section. "They look like they have the kind of uniforms that the army used to wear long ago."

"You're right," Dr. Scott answered, clearly excited. "And look here, in the center must be the general. Good Heavens," he said unbelievingly, "I think this is Custer and the drawing must be an account of the Battle of the Little Big Horn."

"It must be Custer," said William. "See, he is dressed differently than the soldiers. Didn't he wear a buckskin jacket?"

"Where?" Joe asked. "I don't see, which one?"

"Here," Dr. Scott said, putting his finger on the figure, "this one with the long yellow hair." Then pointing to another figure, "And this must be the Indian who shot him. See, he is holding a gun."

There was a mournful wail from Grandma, who covered her face with her hands. She was still afraid.

"How can you tell who it is?" asked Joe. "His face is all covered with what looks like drops of water or blood."

"Rain-in-the-Face," said the historian softly.

He was silent, gazing at the wondering faces around him.

"I won't be sure until I review the information on this battle, but there was a Sioux warrior called

---

5. **pictograph narrative.** Story told by using pictures to represent words or ideas

6. **Winter Count.** Pictograph or picture representation created by Native Americans to keep a record of important yearly events

---

words for everyday use

buck • skin (bək´skin) *n.,* skin of a male deer. *The Revolutionary War soldier wore a uniform made out of buckskin.*

Rain-in-the-Face who was suspected of killing both General Custer and his brother. In fact, if I remember right, I believe he bragged of doing so. But there were many conflicting stories from Indians who were at the Little Big Horn, and those who may have really known, would not say. . . ."

". . . for a hundred years," William finished for him.

"Yes, one hundred years," repeated Dr. Scott. "Did High Elk participate in this battle?" he asked William.

William looked at his mother who had uncovered her eyes. "So my husband was told," she said quietly.

"High Elk must have made this record of the killing of Custer," the historian said, "and then to keep the vow he and other warriors made, he buried it for safekeeping in the cave."

"Did you know of this, *Ina?*" William asked his mother.

She nodded. "My husband told me, whose father told him. I was to tell you before I died."

"This can't be true," Mr. Iron Cloud broke in. "My great-grandfather, who was in this battle, said that Custer killed himself."

"As I said," Mr. Scott looked at Mr. Iron Cloud, "there were so many conflicting stories of what happened on that day. There was also much confusion and a thick dust <u>enveloped</u> the battlefield, making observation difficult."

"What do you suppose this means?" asked Joe, who had been studying the pictures. "This man with antlers on his head, who looks like he's taking funny steps, he's leading a horse—why it looks like Śungwiye." He looked at his father. "Do you think that's supposed to be High Elk leading a horse away from the battlefield?"

"Why, I know about this," Howard said in surprise. "Grandpa told me that near the end of the battle

▶ What does Dr. Scott think the narrative in the bundle depicts?

---

words for everyday use   en • vel • op (in ve´ləp) v., enclose or enfold completely as if with a covering. *As the fog began to <u>envelope</u> our car, it became harder and harder to see the road ahead of us.*

High Elk found the wounded mare and led her to safety. Man, I never thought I would ever see a picture of it."

"Yes," agreed Grandma, "the mare was taken from the soldiers on that day. She was wounded in the leg and lamed after it healed."

◀ What information does Grandma give them?

"I thought he stole the horse from another tribe," Joe said.

At this, his grandmother shook her head, "No. That was the story he told to prevent punishment."

"Didn't the army put big 'U.S.' brands on their stock?" Howard asked Dr. Scott. "I wonder how High Elk kept the soldiers from seeing it."

"Yes," Dr. Scott answered, "the animals were branded. Do you know about this, Mrs. High Elk?" he asked Grandma.

She shook her head.

"But look," Mr. Iron Cloud interrupted. "How could High Elk know who killed Custer if he was leading a horse away from the battleground? See, he has his back to the whole thing."

The group around the table fell silent.

"Gee," Joe said quietly, "this is more mysterious than ever. What *does* it all mean?" he asked, looking at his father and then at Dr. Scott.

Dr. Scott smiled, "It means that you have found a very valuable historical record, even with all its mystery. It is probably worth hundreds or perhaps thousands of dollars, depending on which museum wants it badly enough."

◀ What is the narrative worth?

Wordlessly the family stared at him.

"The horses, the herd . . ." William murmured, thinking of what the money could do.

Dr. Scott began rolling the leather back up. "If it meets with your approval, I would like to take this, and the wrappings, back to the university with me. I need more time to examine it and do a thorough study. When I have done so I will make a public announcement of the discovery. Can I assume you would sell the pictograph?"

William looked at his wife, who smiled at him, then at the tribal chairman. "Frank," he began and then he said to Dr. Scott, "I don't know."

▶ How much can the Tribal Museum spend on the treasure?

Mr. Iron Cloud cleared his throat, "The tribe wouldn't be able to pay you anything, Will, but we would be honored to have this in our new Tribal Museum."

"Well, think about it," said Dr. Scott. "There will be plenty of time in which to make a decision. In the meantime, I will give you a receipt showing that I am borrowing the pictograph from you. I hope you will trust me to take good care of it."

"Dad! Dad!" Marie came screaming into the house. Startled, William leapt to his feet. In his concentration on the unwrapping of the bundle, he hadn't noticed the little girl's absence.

"Dad," she called again. "Śungwiye had her baby. Oh, come see!"

The excited group quickly started to go outside. Marie took her mother's hand.

▶ What did Marie get to watch?

"Mama, I hid behind the shed and peeked, where Śungwiye wouldn't see me. Mama," Marie said, full of wonder, "I saw it born."

"Yahoo!" Joe yelled, following his father out the door. "Come on, Howard," he called to his cousin, "see a new High Elk horse!"

William ran into the shed and knelt by the mare to examine the new foal.

"It is a male," he announced.

Joe was close to tears as he watched Śungwiye gently licking and nuzzling the colt which lay snuggled close to her side. The mare carefully stood and began nudging the perfect little horse to his feet. He struggled to untangle his long, thin legs, not yet sure what they were for. He gained his footing on delicate front hooves, <u>spraddled</u> before him. Śungwiye nudged encouragingly at his rear, and awkwardly, but surely, he stood. He swayed and staggered, staring curiously at the people watching his progress. He took a cautious step, turned to his mother and began to nurse.

---

words for everyday use   **sprad • dle** (spra´dəl) *v.*, sprawl. *I like to <u>spraddle</u> across the sofa to watch my favorite cartoon.*

"Oh, isn't he beautiful," Marie said softly. "Why he looks just like Star."

The colt did resemble his sister. The same golden color, dark now with the wetness of his birth, the same star-shaped blaze on his forehead and four identical white stockings.

"What will we call him?" asked Marie. "He can't be 'Star' too."

"He should have a Lakota name," said Joe. "One that means 'hope' or 'beginning,' because that's what he is, isn't he Dad?"

William nodded, his throat too tight to speak.

"The colt will be called *'Otokahe,'*" said Grandma. "Beginning."

◀ *What does Grandma say the new colt should be named?*

Respond to the Selection

How many new beginnings are there for the High Elk family? Which new beginning do you find the most exciting? Why?

Investigate, Inquire, and Imagine

Recall: GATHERING FACTS

1a. Describe how Howard High Elk looks when he rides up to the High Elk ranch. What problems has Howard experienced? How has he learned about his High Elk heritage?

2a. In the chapter titled, "Joe and Howard," Joe says, "I guess this has been about the most exciting and worried time of my life." Name what worries and excites Joe.

3a. Describe the bundle. What is its condition? How is it wrapped? What is inside?

Interpret: FINDING MEANING

1b. Why do you think Howard and Joe get along so well?

2b. Why does everyone laugh when Joe talks about how worried and excited he has been?

3b. Why did High Elk hide the bundle in the cave? Is the High Elk family honoring High Elk's wishes? Have they waited long enough to open the bundle?

Analyze: TAKING THINGS APART

4a. Explain what is shown in the pictograph narrative. Compare what the family knows about the Battle of Little Big Horn to what the pictograph shows. How do some of the events shown in the narrative differ from what historians say happened? How can Grandma's knowledge help?

Synthesize: BRINGING THINGS TOGETHER

4b. Joe says, "Gee, this is more mysterious than ever." What mysteries does the narrative solve? What mysteries does the narrative not solve? Suggest why the author of *High Elk's Treasure* might leave some mysteries unsolved. What do you suppose Dr. Scott may learn about the narrative?

Evaluate: MAKING JUDGMENTS

5a. What choices do the High Elks have to make about the narrative? Which choice is best, in your opinion?

Extend: CONNECTING IDEAS

5b. Do treasures have to be worth money to be valuable? What treasures do not have price tags?

Understanding Literature

CHARACTER. A **character** is a person or animal who takes part in the action of a literary work. Characters can be classified as major characters or minor characters. *Major characters* are ones who play important roles in a work. *Minor characters* are ones who play less important roles. Joe, the protagonist, is a major character. Who is your favorite minor character in the novel? Why?

SUSPENSE. **Suspense** is a feeling of expectation, anxiousness, or curiosity created by questions raised in the mind of a reader or viewer. Examine how Sneve creates suspense in *High Elk's Treasure.* How many suspenseful events can you identify? How do these events create suspense?

THEME. A **theme** is a central idea in a literary work. It is often found by looking for the meaning behind the things that happen in a story. You usually won't find the theme actually stated in the story, and often a story has more than one theme. What themes did you discover in *High Elk's Treasure?* Which theme do you think is stressed the most? How do events in the story support your choice?

PLOT. A **plot** is a series of events related to a central conflict, or struggle. A plot usually involves the introduction of a conflict, its development and its eventual resolution. The following terms are used to describe the parts of a plot.

The *exposition,* or introduction, sets the tone or mood, introduces the characters and the setting, and provides necessary background information.

The *inciting incident* is the event that introduces the central conflict.

The *climax* is the high point of interest or suspense in the story.

The *resolution* is the point at which the central conflict is ended, or resolved.

The *dénouement* is any material that follows the resolution and that ties up loose ends.

List the series of events in *High Elk's Treasure* that lead to the birth of Śungwiye's new colt. What information did you find in the exposition? What is the inciting incident that first introduces the central conflict? What is the climax? What is the resolution that leads to the ending of all of the conflicts? Why is it important that the new foal is a colt?

Plot Analysis of
High Elk's Treasure

A plot is a series of events related to a central conflict, or struggle. A plot usually involves the introduction of a conflict, its development, and its eventual resolution. The following diagram, known as a plot pyramid, illustrates the main plot of *High Elk's Treasure*. For definitions and more information on the parts of a plot illustrated below, see the Handbook of Literary terms on page 108.

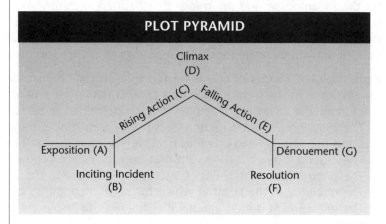

PLOT PYRAMID

Climax
(D)

Rising Action (C)   Falling Action (E)

Exposition (A)   Dénouement (G)

Inciting Incident   Resolution
(B)   (F)

The parts of a plot are as follows:

The **exposition** is the part of a plot that provides background information about the characters, setting, or conflict.

The **inciting incident** is the event that introduces the central conflict.

The **rising action**, or complication, develops the conflict to a high point of intensity.

The **climax** is the high point of interest or suspense in the story.

The **falling action** is all the events that follow the climax.

The **resolution** is the point at which the central conflict is ended or resolved.

The **dénouement** is any material that follows the resolution and that ties up loose ends.

Exposition (A)

As the novel opens, students at an American-Indian elementary school who ride the bus are being sent home because of a severe weather watch. Students who walk or ride to school are allowed to go home if they do not have to cross the creek on their way home. Because eighth-grader Joe High Elk and his ten-year-old sister Marie ride a horse to school and have to cross the creek, their teacher, Mr. Gray Bear, asks them to stay at school. Joe convinces his teacher to allow him and his sister to go home because their stock is out and their grandmother is home alone. Joe does not reveal the specific reason he is in a hurry to get home—he wants to make sure that his horse Šungwiye is safe. Šungwiye is due to have a new foal soon. Horses are very important to the High Elk family. They have only two horses but are trying to recreate a large herd like the one their great-grandfather High Elk once had. Joe and Marie start off for home on their other horse, Star.

Inciting Incident (B)

Just as Joe, Marie, and Star are almost across the shallow creek, a clap of thunder scares Star, who then jumps and slips in the mud. Joe and Marie fall off Star. After making sure that his sister is okay, Joe looks for Star. He is horrified to see that Star is limping. Joe wraps Star's reins around his waist and picks up his sister. He tries to get everyone to a shelter. Joe leads Marie to safety in a cave, but Star is too scared to come into the cave. The horse backs off, loses its footing, slips into the rising creek, and is carried off downstream. Joe sees Star make it safely to the other side of the creek, but then watches her disappear into the trees.

Rising Action (C)

Joe and Marie stay in the cave until the storm is over. Joe, angry with himself, picks up a branch in the cave and starts beating the branch against the cave wall. His beatings create a hole. As Joe tries to fix the hole, he discovers a leather bundle buried in the earthen wall of the cave. Joe believes that the bundle is something that was hidden long ago by his great-grandfather High Elk. Joe carefully removes the bundle and wraps it in Marie's sweater. Joe and Marie take the bundle home.

When Joe and Marie get home, Joe is relieved to see that Śungwiye is safe. When Joe tells his family about the bundle, his grandmother is very worried. Grandma says that the bundle must not be disturbed for one hundred years. Joe's father, William, believes that the bundle has been buried for nearly one hundred years and can be opened, but that they must open the bundle in the presence of an authoritative witness. William also says they must wait to begin the search for Star until they have horses and more help. The High Elks give the bundle to Grandma for safekeeping. The next day the High Elks' kind neighbor, Mr. Blue Shield, helps Joe search for Star. He drives Joe to Bald Peak, where Joe finds that horse catchers have captured Star.

Joe runs back to find Mr. Blue Shield. Joe and Mr. Blue Shield confront the horse catchers. Joe proves that Star is his horse by mounting her without a halter. The horse catchers ride away and Joe rides Star home.

That evening, Joe's father says Dr. Scott, a university historian, and Mr. Iron Cloud, the tribal chairman, will arrive tomorrow to help open the bundle. As Joe and his father are talking, they see someone riding up. The rider is one of the horse catchers—and he is hurt. The rider says that Martin, the mean-looking horse catcher, has knocked him around. The High Elks learn that the rider's name is Howard Anderson and that his mother was a High Elk. The High Elks befriend Howard when they learn about the problems Howard has had at home and at school. Joe and Howard share information about their High Elk heritage. Howard contacts his family and finds that they are relieved and happy to hear from him. In two weeks, Howard's family will come to take him home. Until his family arrives, Howard agrees to help the Blue Shields on their ranch.

Climax (D)

Dr. Scott and Mr. Iron Cloud arrive to witness the opening of the bundle. William invites Howard to join everyone. Dr. Scott carefully unwraps the bundle and discovers that it contains a pictograph narrative. The pictograph shows a scene from the Battle of Little Big Horn. In the pictograph, a man with drops of water on his face points a gun at a yellow-haired figure on the ground. Dr. Scott says that the pictograph may show that a man called Rain-in-the-Face killed General Custer. The pictograph also shows someone, possibly Joe's great-grandfather, leading a horse away from the battle site.

Falling Action (E)

Dr. Scott says he will do a thorough study of the pictograph and make an announcement about its discovery. He also says that the High Elks will receive thousands of dollars if they sell the pictograph to a museum. Mr. Iron Cloud counters that by saying that although the Tribal Museum can't afford to pay anything, it, too, would be honored to display the pictograph.

Resolution (F)

While the adults are discussing what to do, Marie runs in to say that Šungwiye has delivered her foal. Everyone rushes to the shed to see the new foal. They find that the new foal is a colt, or young male horse, who looks just like Star. The High Elks have started to rebuild their herd.

Dénouement (G)

Grandma gives the new foal a Lakota name, *Otokahe,* which means "beginning."

"Completing the Circle"
Virginia Driving Hawk Sneve

ABOUT THE RELATED READING

Virginia Driving Hawk Sneve spent many years searching records and talking to relatives about the history of her family. Her book, *Completing the Circle*, tells what she learned about four generations of women in her family. Each generation dealt with changing traditions and shifting fortunes. In the last chapter of her book, Sneve retells her own story. Part of that chapter is included below. The last chapter, which has the same title as her book, shares what life was like for the Sneves during the Great Depression, a time in the 1930s of great economic hardship. Jobs and the comforts of life were hard for all Americans to find, including those living on Indian reservations.

Completing the Circle

Rose Ross, my mother, completed the eighth grade at the Rosebud Boarding School, and she joined her brother George at the Santee Normal Training School, where their Frazier grandparents had been among the first pupils, and where the Frazier children had been educated. This move to a place far removed from home, and what to Rose was a strange land, was not as traumatic as the first year at the Rosebud Boarding School had been. She was older, toughened by the harsh life at the Rosebud school, and Rose had another comfort.

> ▶ Who is able to comfort the author's mother?

"While I was still at the boarding school, I started keeping steady company with Jimmy, your dad," Rose told me sixty years later. James, the only living child of Robert and Flora Driving Hawk, had planned to finish high school at the Haskell Institute in Lawrence, Kansas, "but he followed me to Santee," where they stayed for three years and were married before they graduated.

The wedding, on 26 May 1932, was performed by the Reverend Paul Barbour, an Episcopal priest, a staunch friend of Flora and Robert Driving Hawk's who would become James's mentor.

The elder Driving Hawks built Rose and Jimmy a two-room house next to their own small home in Mission. I was born in February 1933, and that summer and fall Jimmy worked in a WPA camp[1] in Wyoming with his uncle Dick Clairmont. After his return, Jimmy began studying for the Episcopal priesthood under Father Barbour's tutelage.

My brother Edward was born in 1935, and later that year we moved to Milk's Camp at Ponca Creek, where James had charge of All Saints Episcopal Chapel. The chapel was across the creek from the Congregational church where Hannah and Charles Frazier had lived.

My memories of our stay there are sad and happy, tinged with nostalgia for that short time of being part of a loving family. I was five when I first attended the Milk's Camp Bureau of Indian Affairs Day School. Dad walked me to school and came to get me. We walked along the creek, its smooth running waters reflecting the golden trees. I watched a dry leaf fall into the water and followed it downstream until we cut across a field. In the winter the creek froze solid, and sometimes Dad pushed me on a sled. In the spring we avoided the creek because the low land about it was soggy and muddy. "Stay away from the creek," my brother and I were warned as the placid stream overflowed its banks.

◄ *How does the author get to school?*

We had a dog, a mixed German shepherd we called "Soup" because one member of the congregation teased us that the dog would make good soup when we ran out of food. My brother Eddie had a toy

◄ *Who is Soup?*

---

1. **WPA camp.** Camp operated by a federal government department, the Works Progress Administration, that created jobs for poor Americans

words for everyday use

staunch (stŏnch´) *adj.*, steadfast in loyalty or principle. *Belinda is a staunch friend to Arturo because she helps and supports him whenever he has a problem.*

nos • tal • gia (nä stal´jə) *n.*, longing for something past. *When Benito moved to Chicago, he felt nostalgia for his old neighborhood in San Diego.*

stuffed red rooster that Soup played with. She'd growl and shake it and then drop it at our feet as a signal to throw it so she could retrieve it. She'd dash off with it, and we'd chase her across the prairie, zigging and zagging, but always ending up at home. Soup was our playmate, for we never saw other children save on Sundays and at school. She was our companion on excursions over the prairies to gather wildflowers or to the creek to float stick and leaf boats. Soup stayed with us, never straying to chase rabbits or squirrels, and she knew when it was time to go home. She nipped at our heels and herded us in the right direction, tugging on our clothes if we dawdled.

It was a good place to be a child, but life was not easy at Ponca Creek. My father kept a diary as part of his pastoral duties, and his terse entries began on 21 January 1936: "2 PM. severe blizzard—work on WPA." All the next two years Jimmy was part of an all-male Indian WPA, part of the federal government's national Works Project Administration, which provided jobs to the unemployed. For the next two years Jimmy was part of a repair and painting crew that worked even in the coldest weather. On 3 February he wrote, "WPA. Left side of my <u>countenance</u> froze."

Other entries during those years voice his concern that "Rose and the kids will have enough to eat even though we 'fasted from meat' for several weeks." He wrote of riding into Herrick in a parishioner's wagon to get coal to heat the church and our two-room house. When there was no money to buy fuel, he chopped wood along Ponca Creek.

The dog Soup always accompanied him into the woods. On one such expedition the daylight was fading when Soup came home alone. The dog whined and nipped at Mother's heels and tugged at her dress, just as she did when she wanted Eddie and me to go home. Rose was frantic; she knew something had

▶ *What is life like for Jimmy?*

---

words for everyday use
coun • te • nance (kaunt´ən ənts) *n.,* face, or visage, especially the face as an indication of mood, emotion, or character. *Gabriella's <u>countenance</u> during the storm remained calm.*

happened to Jimmy. She had to follow the dog, so she put Eddie and me to bed, told us not to get up until she got back, and went looking for Jimmy.

Soup led the way to where Jimmy sat dazed in the snow, bleeding from a gash on his head. While he was chopping wood, he had swung the axe up and back, and the heavy iron head had flown off and knocked him down. Rose struggled to get him to his feet and half carried, half led him back to the house. She made Eddie and me get dressed, put on our coats, and bundled us in quilts into the backseat of the car. She managed to get Jimmy in the car, also quilt wrapped, and she drove all night, about three hundred miles, to Okreek, where Eddie and I were left with Grandma Harriet.

◀ How does Rose rescue Jimmy?

Grandpa Ed went on with Rose to Mission, where they made a brief stop to pick up the Driving Hawks, then drove on to the Rosebud hospital, where Jimmy was diagnosed as having a severe concussion.

Rose shivered and shook her head as she recalled the incident. "I've never been so scared. It was so cold—the car heater didn't begin to keep us warm. I prayed the whole way that the old car wouldn't break down. I guess I could have taken Jimmy to the doctor in Bonesteel, but I wanted to get home."

Rose had no family or close friends in Milk's Camp to go to for help. She was lonely at Ponca Creek, although I didn't know it then. Jimmy was often away at his WPA jobs or responding to a middle-of-the-night summons because of the illness or death of some member of his congregation. When word came about Rose's sister Alma's tragic death as the result of an exploding stove, I vividly remember Rose weeping with deep <u>wrenching</u> sobs as she sat on the steps of our little house with only Eddie and me trying to comfort her. "Don't cry, Mama," we urged, patting and hugging her. We didn't understand how she could weep so, and we were frightened to see her distress.

◀ What is life like for Rose?

---

words for everyday use   **wrench** (rench´) *n.*, sudden tug at one's emotions. *Sam felt a <u>wrench</u> in his stomach when he learned that his grandmother had died.* **wrenching,** *adj.*

But most of my memories of Ponca Creek are happy ones. I was innocently unaware of our poverty; I don't recall ever being hungry or cold.

I remember going with Mother to the ladies' extension classes at the Milk's Camp Day School, where a white female agent showed the women how to prepare the commodity foods[2] issued to the Indians during the depression. Once, I was happily stuffed with grapefruit, part of the commodity ration that the congregation didn't like and gave to us.

Our life was centered around church activities and the day school, which was also the Milk's Camp community center. Periodically, we went there to get commodities issued from the school warehouse. In the summer we'd help weed and hoe the large community garden planted on the school grounds. Dad helped with the harvest; then we'd stay at home with him while Mom helped process the vegetables in the cannery. She'd come home with a box of canned corn, green beans, and other vegetables—our part of the produce, which each family shared.

Community meetings were held at the school, which also served as the polling place for the newly <u>enfranchised</u> Indians. The whole community came to see the children perform in the Christmas program, and Jimmy went there once a week to give religious education before such instruction was banned. This was where, when only five, I started the first grade and learned to read. Reading came easily to me, and I came to love words, which let my mind soar into a universe I had never known was there. Mr. Miller, my first teacher, was delighted and encouraged by my <u>fledgling</u> flights with books from his personal library.

▶ What does the author do in the summer?

---

2. **commodity foods.** Agricultural products such as cheese, meat, and canned goods distributed by the government

words for everyday use

en • fran • chise (in fran´chīz) v., give full privileges of citizenship to; especially to give the right to vote. *Congress enacted a law in 1870 that <u>enfranchised</u> black citizens.*

fledg • ling (flej´liŋ) n., one that is new. *My dad's <u>fledgling</u> company is making a profit in its first year.*

Sundays, of course, the people came to church. Mother played the organ, making sure that Eddie and I were seated on the front pew by the organ, where she could keep an eye on us. I stayed put, enjoying the music and singing Lakota even though I didn't understand the words. However, as soon as Mother started pumping the organ and her hands were busy on the keys, Eddie escaped, crawling under the pews, over kneelers and people's feet—all the way to the rear and out the door.

◀ What does the family do on Sundays?

Winyan Omniciye, the women's guild, met in the members' homes, but other gatherings were held in our house, which had one large kitchen–living room and one small bedroom. Some nights I'd fall asleep to the close harmonic tones of "Skeeters am a humming on the honey suckle vine . . ." of the Milk's Camp barbershop quartet, who practiced at our house. Asampi, Chief Milk, was dead then, but his grandson sang baritone to my father's tenor.

Sometimes during the night, I'd awaken to radio music and my parents' laughter as they danced to big band sounds. The battery-powered radio brought drama and humor into our home with Fibber McGee, the Lone Ranger, Ma Perkins, and other radio plays, to which I created pictures in my mind. But we liked the music best.

Dad had learned to play the trombone in school, and I'd tease him to play for me; sometimes he would, but not too often because some member of the congregation was always dropping in. Music was important to him; in fact, he played trombone with the reservation dance band, Chief Crazy Horse and the Syncopators, "but I'm not enjoying it, so much, so I guess those days are over for me," he wrote in 1936.

After we moved to Okreek, I took piano lessons and felt so grown up accompanying Dad's trombone improvisations—until his lips got sore. Then he'd

◀ What musical things does the author's father do?

---

words for everyday use

im • prov • i • sa • tion (im präv ə zā´shən) *n.*, act of composing, reciting, or singing without preparation. *Greta's improvisation at the party showed us how well she could act even without rehearsing.*

shake his head, wipe his mouth, and put the horn away. Mrs. Red Buffalo was shocked when she came into the house unannounced to find Jimmy teaching me to dance to music from the radio.

After I learned to play the organ, some Sundays Dad would take me with him to the reservation chapels that he served. My legs were barely long enough for my feet to pump the pedals, but I began being a church organist. I also began learning to drive on those Sundays in the fall so that Dad could hunt pheasant on the way to and from the chapels.

James's diaries are daily recordings of his pastoral duties, with rare notations of a personal item. In June 1942, he made a brief mention of our trip to the Black Hills with stops at Wind Cave, Iron Mountain, Mount Rushmore, and Rapid City. My memory of that trip is not of the Black Hills but of an incident en route that I later included in an essay, "Special Places" (1978).

▶ Why is travel hazardous?

Travel during wartime was a hazardous adventure on old patched tires and gas rationing.[3] It was hot, and our old Chevy had a canvas water bag tied to the front of the radiator in case the car overheated and for drinking when we got thirsty. I had a stomachache in anticipation of the adventures ahead.

We had been holding our breath for miles, praying that the few drops of gasoline left in the tank would get us to the next town and a gas station. I had to go to the toilet again. Dad complained at the frequency of my need, which called for many stops and a run for the ditch. So I was doubly glad to see the gas station and hoped for the privacy of a privy and maybe even running water.

While the car was at the pump, I ran to the back of the station and saw three doors: MEN, WOMEN, INDIANS.

---

3. **gas rationing.** Regulating the amount of gas people may purchase, done when gas is in short supply

words for everyday use

en • route (än rüt´) adv., on or along the way. Carlos was en route to his aunt's house when the accident happened.

WOMEN was locked, so I rushed into INDIANS, trying not to breathe the foul air or sit on the soiled stool.

As we resumed the journey, I thought about the three doors. "That gas station had three rest rooms," I told my parents. "One for men, one for women, and one for Indians."

I remember Mom and Dad looking at each other as I went on, "Isn't it nice that there was a special place for Indians?"

No one said anything for a while; then Dad patted my knee. "My girl, I hope there will always be special places for you."

Years later, when I was aware of the bigotry and prejudice that existed outside my secure family, I remembered Dad's words. I learned that I had to create my own "special places" because no one else would provide them.

◀ What does the author learn about the treatment of Indians?

Okreek was a special place for me. I was pleased that the house we lived in had an upstairs with one side that I could call "my room." I could be by myself to read and dream. It wasn't much more than an attic, but it became the garret of Louisa May Alcott's little women and Dickens's London.

I remember Christmases in Okreek, although I wished we could have our own Christmas tree. There was one tall tree in the guild hall,[4] but it was for the whole congregation. On Christmas Eve old and young gathered in the hall for a meal and gifts. The tree was trimmed with handkerchiefs, which were gifts for the men and women. Every child got an apple, an orange, and a paper bag full of candy, and as the excited young ones clutched the fruit and dug into the candy, loud stomps and a deep bass "Ho, ho, ho!" were heard at the door.

"Sh, sh," the adults commanded. "Listen! What's that?"

Round-eyed children crept close to mothers as the door opened and with a gust of cold air Santa Claus came in. Some children screamed with fright, never in their life ever seeing such a figure, all in red, and a bushy white beard. But Santa calmed them with

---

4. **guild hall.** Room or hall in a church where people gather

soothing Lakota and gave each child a ball, top, car, or doll.

Then we all walked up the hill to Calvary Church for the midnight service. It was a mystical place at night, with swags of greenery and lots of candles, for there were no electric lights. Carols, sung in Lakota, rang through the night, but I rarely managed to stay awake for the whole service. At its end, we'd stumble down through snow to a cold house and beds, for we'd never leave a fire in the wood stove when no one was there.

The next morning Grandma and Grandpa Ross joined us, Robert and Flora Driving Hawk having come the night before, and we opened our family gifts before Jimmy had to drive off to the chapel at Ideal for the Christmas service there.

▶ What is in the Mission boxes?

Some of our gifts were clothing that came in the Mission boxes sent from wealthy Episcopal churches in New England. It was an exciting time when the boxes came, for I helped unpack. Often I'd find a glamorous ball gown with "jewels" or one of slinky velvet. Sometimes there were shiny worn dress coats with funny tails and white bibs and black bow ties. The adults would laugh at the impracticality of such articles of clothing, but when Mother let me wear them, it was fun to play dress up and become a <u>debutante</u>.

Mission box time was also disappointing because we never got first pick of the practical dresses, under-wear, trousers, shirts, shoes, and coats. "The people need them, more than we do," Mom gently explained.

One fall I had grown so tall so fast that my winter coat was too small. I prayed for a just-my-size coat to come in a mission box—the same place I'd gotten my present coat the year before, only then the sleeves hung over my fingers, leaving growing room. Now, the hemline came above my knees, my wrists stuck

---

words for everyday use   deb • u • tante (deb´yù tänt) n., young woman making a formal entrance into society. *When Robert's grandmother was young, she was a <u>debutante</u> in Boston.*

out like skinny sticks, and the coat was tight over my shoulders.

The boxes came, and there was the most beautiful coat I had ever seen. It was a smooth, grayish, soft fur. "Ooh," I tried it on, <u>enthralled</u> with its sleek warmth. It was perfect—only a little long, and I could wrap it around me twice. But with all my heart I wanted that coat. Of course, I couldn't have it, but every day I came home from school and checked to see whether it was still hanging in the rummage room. Then it was gone, and I was heartbroken.

◀ What is the coat like?

The next day, it was cold and rainy. I miserably donned my old coat, tied on a scarf, and pulled on mittens, but there were four inches of bare skin between mitten and sleeve. It was a bitter walk to school. I took my coat to the cloakroom, and there, hanging on the first hook, was the fur coat. It wasn't until school was out that I found out who had claimed the fur. It was a cold, wet walk in the rain. All the Episcopal kids were going to the guild hall for the weekly youth meeting, and Pauline Wright walked beside me in the fur coat.

"I'm so glad I got this *new* coat," she said. (I thought she gloated.) "It's so warm and keeps me dry. Aren't you cold?"

Miserably I nodded my head, but said nothing about her *new fur coat*. But I saw out of the corner of my eye that it almost dragged on the ground and that its hem was wet and splashed with mud.

In the guild hall we stood near the wood stove to warm ourselves before the meeting. Soon a dank aroma filled the room as our damp coats steamed and dried. "Phew," one of the boys said. "Pauline, your coat smells like a wet dog," and everyone laughed.

◀ Why is the author glad that she doesn't get the coat?

I was glad that I wasn't wearing that coat, and Pauline, embarrassed by the "wet dog" remark, never wore it again.

---

words for everyday use

en • thrall (in thrôl´) v., hold by or as if by a spell. *Glenda's stories could <u>enthrall</u> audiences for hours.*

Critical Thinking

1. Compare Sneve's real life to the life of Joe High Elk. What things are the same in their lives? What things are different?

2. Examine events in Sneve's life. What kind of attitude does she have toward life? Do you think she had a happy childhood? Why, or why not? What type of events does she remember most? What factors may determine whether or not one has a happy childhood?

3. Describe Sneve's parents. What was life like for each of them? How do you think their lives affected Sneve's views about life? What values did they instill in their children?

4. Who was Mr. Miller and why was he important in Sneve's life? Do you think he influenced Sneve to become a writer and teacher? Why, or why not?

"Family Treasures, Family Pleasures"
Lila Perl

ABOUT THE RELATED READING

Lila Perl grew up in Brooklyn, New York. When her children were young, she volunteered to help an elementary class gather information about their ancestry and was amazed at the students' interest in the subject. This reading selection is taken from her book, *The Great Ancestor Hunt,* a book that helps children dig into their family's roots. Perl believes that finding out more about one's ancestors helps build "a sense of 'belonging' in a rapidly changing world."

Family Treasures, Family Pleasures

An old wedding dress with a veil of yellow lace, a pair of baby shoes of crinkled white leather, a first-grade report card, a handmade Valentine, a dried and faded flower from a <u>corsage</u> worn to a high school prom. . . . Are there possessions like these tucked away in a drawer, a closet, an attic storeroom in your home, or that of a close relative? Often such bits of personal and family <u>memorabilia</u> are tattered and brittle. They may be of no value to the outside world. Yet, among all the items that pass through our hands day after day, somebody chose to save these particular ones.

The places that these keepsakes have been, the people who have seen or handled them, the feelings they have evoked are all part of the story they tell. For four generations, one family has kept and displayed a

words for everyday use	cor • sage (kȯr säzh´) *n.,* arrangement of flowers worn as a fashion accessory. *Melinda's sister wore a <u>corsage</u> of tiny flowers to the dance.*	mem • o • ra • bil • ia (me mə rə bi´lē ə) *n.,* things that are remarkable and worthy of remembrance. *My mother has saved <u>memorabilia</u> from every one of my elementary school classes.*

framed needlework sampler.[1] Its center is embroidered[2] in many-colored threads with a pattern of a peacock surrounded by leaves and flowers. At the top of the embroidery are the initials *S.K.* and, at the bottom, the date *1895,* all worked in cross-stitch.[3]

Samplers similar to this one began to be made as early as the 1500s. Young girls and women embroidered the letters of the alphabet, numbers, verses, sayings, and pictures on cloth to show examples—or "samples"—of their skill with various needlework stitches. Sometimes they added their initials, their age, or the date, making a sampler a meaningful family "document" as well as a family treasure.

Who was the S.K. whose handiwork was passed on from one generation to the next? Where was she in 1895, and what thoughts did she have as she sat with her embroidery before her? Her story is one of loneliness and fear of abandonment. But it is also one that has a happy ending.

At the time she made her sampler, S.K. was a young married woman with an infant daughter. She was living in a poor village in northwestern Russia. Six months earlier, her young husband, due to be taken into the czar's[4] army, which was <u>notorious</u> for its harsh treatment of Jews, had left Russia in the dark of night. Now he was in America, rooming with strangers in a tenement flat and trying to find steady work as a tailor. He was living on bakery rolls and coffee for pennies a day in order to save enough money to bring his wife and baby over from Europe.

Young <u>emigrant</u> men such as he were sometimes known to vanish into the crowded cities across the sea, never to be heard from again. Others took many years to send for their families. Often husbands and

▶ *What things do girls embroider on samplers?*

---

1. **sampler.** Decorative piece of needlework
2. **embroidered.** Decorated with needlework
3. **cross-stitch.** Needlework stitch that forms an *X*
4. **czar's.** Belonging to ruler in Russia; czars reigned until the 1917 revolution

---

words for everyday use

no • tor • i • ous (nō tôr′ē əs) *adj.,* generally known and talked of. *Michael Jordan is a <u>notorious</u> basketball player because he made so many amazing baskets.*

em • i • grant (e′mi grənt) *n.,* departing or having departed from a country to settle elsewhere. *Hamzi was an <u>emigrant</u> from Egypt.*

wives were strangers when at last they met once more. Would S.K., who was herself an orphan, be left to the uncertainties and dangers of Jewish life in czarist Russia? The fact that this great-great-grandmother's embroidered sampler has been in America for close to a century tells us that she *was* reunited with her husband and lived out her life here after all.

◀ What happens to S.K. and her husband?

In another family, there may not be a sampler that tells a story. But there may be an old pieced-together quilt that crossed the plains, bits of hand-made lace, a knitted or crocheted shawl or afghan[5] from a beloved grandmother. There may be keepsakes such as ringlets of baby hair, <u>souvenirs</u> in the form of old ticket stubs and theater programs, "found" objects like a collection of seashells or rock samples from a memorable outing or vacation. There may be medals, awards, or trophies recalling honors bestowed in days gone by. Often, too, there are family <u>heirlooms</u>—a gold locket, a crystal vase, a pair of silver candlesticks.

◀ What other keepsakes do people save?

What would any of these articles say if they could speak to us? Unlocking the secrets within these "treasures" may be as simple as asking questions of older relatives about them. By combining the answers with your other family-history notes, you will be enriching and illuminating *your* family's heritage. You will also have made a valuable record for generations to come.

Among other treasures that families hold onto are those made of paper. They range from family bibles to old diaries, letters, and scrapbooks; from baby-record books to high-school autograph albums; from birth announcements to college diplomas; from wedding invitations to death certificates.

◀ What kind of paper treasures are saved?

---

5. **afghan.** Blanket or shawl of colored wool

words for everyday use

sou • ven • ir (sū və nir´) *n.,* something that serves as a reminder. *Lizzie brought back a souvenir from her trip to Disneyland.*

heir • loom (ar´lūm) *n.,* piece of property that descends to the heir as part of an inheritance of property. *Andy's grandmother says her silver teapot is an heirloom she received from her aunt.*

An old family bible can be especially useful in providing clues for ancestor hungers. Starting in the late 1700s, it became the custom for young couples to receive bibles as wedding gifts. On the blank first page or pages, they recorded their marriage, the births of their children, and other family events such as baptisms, confirmations, and deaths. As it traveled through the years and accumulated more information, the bible grew into an outline of the family's history.

Other paper treasures tell us of the pride our <u>immigrant</u> ancestors took in acquiring official documents with their names on them. To be the owner of a passport, of "working papers,"[6] and especially of "citizenship papers" was a mark of having become "somebody," of establishing an identity for oneself in the new land.

Back in the early 1900s, for example, many immigrants entered the United States with <u>forged</u> or borrowed passports. Valid passports were often difficult to obtain and cost money that poor families could ill afford.

▶ What does a proper passport allow a person to do?

A proper passport, however, gave one permission to leave one's country of birth legally and to travel through other countries under the protection of the home country. So an immigrant who arrived in America with a government-issued passport from Russia, Italy, Greece, or some other foreign nation was especially proud to be starting out with a genuine passport in hand. No wonder such documents were carefully preserved in families long after their usefulness had ended.

A next step in an immigrant family might be for one of the children to apply for "working papers." In New York City in the early 1900s, young people were allowed to leave school and look for a full-time job at

---

6. **working papers.** Papers that indicate where a person works

words for everyday use

im • mi • grant (i´mi grənt) *n.*, person who comes to a country to take up permanent residence. *Nadia is an immigrant who came to America to start a new life.*

forge (fōrj´) *v.*, make or imitate falsely. *Never forge your father's signature on a note to school or you may get a call from the principal.*

fourteen. Education was important, but so was the need to help out with the family's income and also have a little pocket money of one's own. So, many youngsters never went on to high school. With a grade-school education, they trudged the city's streets seeking almost any kind of work in a factory, store, or warehouse to start them on the road to earning a living. The bright yellow Employment Certificate from the Board of Health was an immigrant teenager's ticket of admission to adulthood and independence.

◀ Why don't many young people go on to high school?

Even more eventful than a first job was the day on which an immigrant became a citizen of the United States. By going through the process known as "naturalization,"[7] a foreigner could be granted the same rights of citizenship as a "natural-born"[8] American. The applicant had to meet several requirements. One of the necessary steps for an immigrant was to have lived in the United States continuously for five years.

◀ What is naturalization?

It was, and still is, the dream of most immigrants to one day take the oath of loyalty to their adopted country and to share in the rights and privileges that country offers its people. Among the valued documents in your family's collection, there is very likely to be a relative's certificate of naturalization, popularly known as "citizenship papers."

A family's memories of itself are made of much more, of course, than old documents and pieces of antique needlework. Meaningful as those memorabilia may be, they don't tell the whole story. For family history is also living history—and even history in the making.

The next time your family gets together for a holiday dinner, a birthday party, or some other special occasion, listen carefully for the shared expressions, jokes, songs, and stories that make your family unique, different in character from all other families.

---

7. **naturalization.** Process that makes a person a citizen of a new country
8. **natural-born.** Person born in this country

Does somebody *always* tell about the time fussy old Great-Uncle Horace took five little nieces and nephews on an ice cream outing and was so fearful they would misbehave that he suggested they be given "spankings in advance"? Is father *always* reminded of the time he was three years old and called grandpa's <u>pompous</u> Cousin Jacques "dummy-head"? Sent to his room as a punishment, he later voiced his innocence with the excuse "I just didn't know his name."

▶ What kind of food stories might a family recall?

Every family has its recipes, its eating traditions, and its occasional food and cooking disasters to recall. There was the time the spaghetti sauce was left on the stove too long and was burnt black, the time the party sandwiches were stolen from the church basement by neighborhood mischief-makers, the time the dog ate the anniversary cake.

There are the wonderful-tasting dishes to remember, like grandma's feather-light dumplings with chicken stew. And the not-so-great ones, like Great-Aunt Sophie's deviled-tongue croquettes.[9] And there are the special holiday food traditions that the family has always observed, like having a velvety egg-and-lemon soup on Easter Eve or a turkey stuffed with pecans and cornbread on Thanksgiving.

▶ What is a family's folklore?

All of these customs and remembrances make up what we call our family's <u>folklore</u>. In the very act of laughing, sighing, or nodding over the shared experiences that bind us, we are not just reliving the past. We are also reinventing it. We are creating new folkloric experiences that will be recalled with pleasure at future family get-togethers.

Unlike the dates, places, and other hard facts we look for in filling in a family-history chart, the subject matter of family folklore doesn't have to be fixed

---

9. **croquettes.** Small round mass of minced meat, fish, or vegetables coated with egg and bread crumbs and deep-fried

words for everyday use

pom • pous (pŏm´pəs) *adj.*, excessively elevated or ornate. *The woman on the train had a pompous attitude when she told the conductor she wouldn't share her seat.*

folk • lore (fō´klōr) *n.*, traditional customs, sayings, tales, dances, or art forms preserved among a people. *Scottish folklore says that bagpipes should be played at funerals.*

or exact. Each time a story is told, it may be changed a little by the teller, who brings something of himself or herself to it. Family folklore lives and grows. Some old tales inevitably fade away, and new stories, or new versions of old stories, are woven into this informal collection.

Family get-togethers are also a wonderful time for asking our relatives what their lives were like when they were our age. What were the clothes and hair styles of the day? What music did they enjoy? What were their favorite toys, games, pastimes, and hobbies? How did they spend their summer vacations? How were things different from today?

◄ What is a good time to ask relatives about what their lives used to be like?

A grandmother tells about growing up in the years before World War II, when there was no TV, there were no plastics, and—worst of all—no antibiotics or polio vaccines. The polio epidemic of the 1930s, she recalls, was an especially scary time. Everyone was terrified of catching the disease. So she and her family spent summers at a country hotel, far away from the crowds of the city. And she shows a picture of a children's masquerade party[10] taken at that hotel, with adult guests looking on from the balcony above. It's hard to imagine your grandmother at six, in a crepe-paper dress[11] and a big hair bow. But there she is.

Does your grandfather have a favorite story about when he was a young man? Perhaps he has described to you his "secret" sailing to Europe on a giant troop carrier during World War II. Nobody was allowed to know when one of the faster ships, its portholes blackened,[12] set out across the Atlantic without an escort, hoping to outrun the German submarines. As the wartime posters read, "Loose lips sink ships!" Can you picture your grandfather at eighteen going to war aboard that ship—one of fifteen thousand men in enough space for half that number, sleeping in eight-hour rotation shifts and washing up in heated salt water?

---

10. **masquerade party.** Party where people wear costumes
11. **crepe-paper dress.** Dress made of paper with a crinkled or puckered texture
12. **portholes blackened.** Covered windows on a ship; windows are often covered during wartime to make sure that no light can escape from the windows and be seen by enemy planes

Or does your grandparent have an experience to relate of life during the Holocaust, the Nazi annihilation of six million Jews? How did he or she avoid dying in the gas chambers of the German concentration camps, as did other family members? Jewish children were sometimes hidden by brave and kindly people, or were sent away to safety in countries not under Nazi domination. But many actually spent time in concentration camps and weren't <u>liberated</u> until World War II ended in Europe.

Stories of narrow escapes in wartime, of heroic acts of rescue, of natural disasters like floods and tornados, of tragically lost opportunities all make up the drama of our families' rememberings.

Happily, there are also the less serious tales that are recalled over and over again. They may be about the romantic twists and turns of a courtship; about how a great fortune was *almost* made by some enterprising relative; or about an old family superstition or a supernatural happening that is sworn to be true. And there are the lighthearted, even <u>giddy</u>, <u>reminiscences</u> of the pranks and practical jokes played on or by family members.

▶ *What other things might a family collect?*

Lastly, almost all families have a collection of special words and phrases that are part of their folklore. Some are expressions that have been handed down by older relatives. Others come directly out of the mispronounced words of young children.

We can't help laughing as we learn that our father "talked funny" when he was little and said things like "pizghetti," for spaghetti, until he was seven years old. Or that our mother used to say "chicken pops" for chicken pox and, for quite a long time, thought they were something good to eat.

What about our own baby words? We all love to hear stories about "when we were little," and they, too, become part of our family's folklore. Which of us didn't have a favorite "blankie" or a tattered "teddy" that had to be sneaked into the wash? What was the special song, story, or "good-night" <u>ritual</u> that could always be counted on to put us to sleep? What can we learn, through the rememberings of our families, about a time that is hidden from us behind the haze of babyhood?

As the search for our roots—both our family's and our own—goes on, we probably will find that we are building up quite a collection of material. Is there some ideal way of "getting it all together" in a form that is also going to be convenient for "passing it on"?

The choice of how to preserve our personal time-lines, direct-ancestry charts, family-interview notes, and much more is really our own. Some of us may prefer a looseleaf notebook or a folder in which to keep our findings. Others may choose to make up a scrapbook with accompanying photographs. We may also have old home movies, tape recordings, and even videotapes that bring our family's history and folklore together, as well as the writings, documents, and keepsakes of our ancestors. So a large, sturdy box or even a small chest may be the answer.

◀ How can you preserve your family's history?

It's a good idea, too, to photocopy all written and printed materials in case the originals are lost. And old family pictures can be photographed, giving us new photos and a set of negatives as well.

One of the great pleasures of being the family "historian" is that of sharing what you've learned. You can do this by starting a family club, circulating a family newsletter, or helping to arrange a family reunion. It's not at all unlikely that your efforts will be rewarded by finding relatives who have also been working on your family's story and who can add to what you already know.

◀ How can you share your family's history?

---

words for everyday use

rit • u • al (ri′chə wəl) *n.*, customarily repeated. *It is a <u>ritual</u> in our family for everyone to take a bath every night.*

In some unforeseen way, working on your heritage may even lead you into a career choice you otherwise might not have dreamed of. Getting "hooked" on family history and family-story material could result in your becoming a genealogist[13] specializing in tracing family lines for individuals or for medical or legal personnel; a library or museum archivist[14] working with public records and historical documents; a researcher of the oral history traditions of various world cultures; a biographer, journalist, photographer, or documentary film-maker.

But even if *all* that happens as a result of your ancestor hunt is that your "sense of family" is awakened and broadened, you will have become richer for the experience.

Your hope of proving that your family owns an <u>authentic</u> coat of arms—an insignia[15] worn in the tournaments and Crusades of the Middle Ages—probably will be dashed. The same may be true of your dreams of finding yourself related to an American president or a superstar of the entertainment world. You may have failed to discover your grandmother's maiden name *or* her secret remedy for curing everything from hiccups to hives. You may not even have been able to find out where in Africa, Asia, Latin America, or Europe your family originally lived.

▶ What might be the main achievement of your family-roots research?

In fact, the main achievement of your family-roots research may be your *own* life story, told in a timeline, notebook, photo scrapbook, diary, or other personal-history format. The value of recording what you've learned about yourself and those who are part of your everyday life is considerable. In finding out who you are, you are putting together an offering

---

13. **genealogist.** Person who traces or studies the descent of persons or families
14. **archivist.** Person in charge of old records
15. **insignia.** Badge of authority or honor

that will strengthen the ties between the present and the future.

Above all, what you've been doing in hunting ancestors is "talking family." In drawing together with those who are closest to you, you have brightened *your* family's "moment" in human history with caring and love.

Critical Thinking

1. Why might it be difficult to save paper records such as photographs and newspaper clippings? How does your family save items such as these?
2. Record some of the things your family does to celebrate holidays, birthdays, and other special occasions. Why are these things important?
3. Ancestors of Native Americans did not move to America; they were already here. Many of them, however, were forced to move to another part of America. How might this have affected their feelings toward newcomers? Why did your family move to America? How were they treated when they arrived? How are newcomers to America treated today?
4. Find out how many of your classmates used the words "pizghetti" and "chicken pops" when they were younger. How many had a sibling with a "blankie" and a "binkie," or pacifier? What other special word memories do you and your classmates have? Are there a lot of memories you share with your classmates? Make a classroom chart that lists special words and phrases that are part of your class's family folklore.

Grandmother Poems

ABOUT THE RELATED READINGS

Grandmothers are highly revered in Native American cultures. They are a source of knowledge, wisdom, and healing. Sneve says, "My grandmothers—and all Indian grandmothers—were better than mothers because, whereas an Indian woman's first duty was to the needs of her husband, grandmothers saw to the needs of their grandchildren." As you can see from the collection of poems here, grandmothers are a common subject for many Native American poems.

Looking for My Old Indian Grandmother in the Summer Heat of 1980
Diane Glancy

The heat uncovers the window and attic-fan
that pulls in more heat.

> ▶ What is the air like when the speaker's grandmother dies?

It was like this in fifty-four, they say,
and I remember, somehow, the hot, white air in the
percale curtains[1] at the window.

It comes back to me now.
I think it was the year my grandmother died.

I look into the trunk, and under the rock
that is her grave.
It was in 1954. July 14.

Her hands and face turn hard before we arrive.
We are bleached clean from her responsibility.

It all happened before I was old enough to ask,
before she knew I would even want to know.

> ▶ Why does the speaker want to know more about her grandmother?

It is because I am more like her than the others
I want to know what rock it is
she left upturned.

---

1. **percale curtains.** Curtains made from fine, closely woven cotton cloth

grandmother
Ray A. Young Bear

if i were to see
her shape from a mile away
i'd know so quickly
that it would be her.
the purple scarf
and the plastic
shopping bag.
if i felt
hands on my head
i'd know that those
were her hands
warm and damp
with the smell
of roots.
if i heard
a voice
coming from
a rock
i'd know
and her words
would flow inside me
like the light
of someone
stirring ashes
from a sleeping fire
at night.

◄ *What are the
grandmother's
hands like?*

I Watched an Eagle Soar
Virginia Driving Hawk Sneve

Grandmother,
I watched an eagle soar
high in the sky
until a cloud covered him up.
Grandmother,
I still saw the eagle
behind my eyes.

▶ Where does the speaker of the poem still see an eagle?

Critical Thinking

1. What kind of relationships do the speakers in each poem have with their grandmothers? Briefly discuss how close each speaker seems to be to his or her grandmother. What words used in the poems lead you to your beliefs?

2. Close your eyes as your teacher or a classmate reads each of the poems. What does each grandmother look like or what do you learn about each grand-mother's personality? Which grandmother do you see most clearly?

"Horse and Native American: The Relationship Begins"
GaWaNi Pony Boy

ABOUT THE RELATED READING

This selection from *Out of the Saddle: Native American Horsemanship* focuses on the relationship that Native Americans have had with horses. The author, GaWaNi Pony Boy, learned about Native American riding skills when he traveled around the United States with a Native American drum group. Pony Boy now teaches children and adults how to ride and understand horses. His methods are based on what he learned in his early travels.

Horse and Native American: The Relationship Begins

Native Americans respect and admire every bird, fish, rock, and plant just as you respect and admire close family members. If you have ever had a long-term relationship with an animal, you probably know the love that grows with this relationship. Horses have been viewed by Native Americans as companions and animals to be cared for. And sometimes the horse was also a messenger, teacher, or guide.

◀ *How have Native Americans viewed horses?*

Native Americans lived for thousands of years without horses. Let's go back in time and find out how Native Americans first met the horse.

Ancestors of the horse lived in North America 40 million years ago. But 15,000 years ago during the Ice Age, the last of these <u>prehistoric</u> animals crossed a land bridge from what is now Alaska to Siberia. There, on the other side of the Pacific Ocean, they roamed over the grasslands of Asia and were domesticated.

words for everyday use pre • his • tor • ic (prē his tōr´ik) *adj.,* of or existing in times before written history. *Prehistoric dinosaurs lived on the land before humans did.*

▶ How did horses get to North America?

Eventually, these domesticated horses were traded westward across Europe and North Africa. When the Spaniards came to explore the New World, they loaded horses onto boats and brought them to North America. Explorers Christopher Columbus, Ponce de León, and Hernando de Soto all brought horses with them.

▶ What animal transported goods before the horse?

Before horses were brought back to North America, Native Americans used dogs in everyday life. Dogs are loyal, good hunters, and they helped transport family belongings. Although Native Americans were never true nomads, some tribes moved from a summer camp to a winter camp. When moving, two large sticks were crossed and tied to a dog's back forming a travois on which family belongings could be tied.

Using dogs for moving wasn't easy. Can you imagine packing all your family's belongings and loading them onto a travois tied to your dog's back instead of getting a moving van? A dog can pack 30 to 40 pounds at best, and walk only 5 to 6 miles per day. And a dog needs to eat meat. Besides that, dogs often fight with each other, and if a rabbit should run across the path, a dog—along with all of his <u>cargo</u>— would take off after it.

The Native American Meets the Horse

▶ What were some early names for horses?

When Native Americans first saw horses, they described them as being giant dogs. Throughout the Nations, the horse was called big dog, medicine dog, elk dog, spirit dog, and mysterious dog. Gradually, several Indian tribes began to understand the strange animals by watching how the Spaniards used them. But when Native Americans in New Mexico drove out the Spanish settlers and captured their sheep, cattle, and horses, they questioned the horses's value. After all, horses ate what little grass there was available for sheep. And it was the sheep, not horses, who could

---

words for everyday use

car • go (kär´gō) *n.*, goods or merchandise conveyed in a ship, airplane, or vehicle. *The heavy load of <u>cargo</u> carried by the barges made them sink low into the water.*

provide meat and wool. So the Southwestern tribes traded the horses to tribes in the north and east.

Many horses escaped <u>captivity</u> and migrated to an area that is now Idaho, Oregon, and Washington. Horses lived well in this region. Snowcapped mountains served as a natural fence line, guarding horses against such enemies as wolves and puma.[1] All around were fields of green grass and mountain streams, so the horses had plenty to eat and drink.

Native peoples in these areas immediately saw how to use the horse to make life easier. A horse can carry 200 pounds on his back or drag 300 pounds on a travois. A horse can travel more than 20 miles a day and needs only grass to eat. And horses are relatively peaceful among themselves. Once tamed, horses are more dependable, easier to handle, and require less care than do dogs.

◄ *How many pounds can a horse carry on a travois?*

With the introduction of the horse, Native American life changed dramatically. On horseback, buffalo could be chased and hunted with great speed, increasing a hunter's chance of success. Hunting territories expanded with the increased ability to track, chase, and successfully hunt buffalo. Riderless horses were used as runners. Runners were trained to run, or chase, a herd of buffalo in the direction of the hunters while the hunters waited atop fresh mounts.

The Shoshoni tribe in Idaho was one of the first to see the value of having horses, but the Nez Percé quickly caught on. An unlikely people to even want horses because the Nez Percé mainly fished for salmon in the beautiful, clear north rivers, they simply liked the horse—especially the spotted ones. So some villages combined their resources and bought several from the Shoshoni.

The Nez Percé didn't waste any time. They began breeding their top mares with their top stallions.

---

1. **puma.** Cougar, a large and powerful brown wild cat of the Americas

---

words for everyday use   cap • tiv • i • ty (kap tiv´və tē) *n.,* state of being captive. *Elephants kept in <u>captivity</u> are not free to search for the food they want.*

▶ What kind of horse did the Nez Percé want?

They wanted horses who were not only swift and surefooted but also calm and even-tempered. This was important in open country where there were no corrals or fences. This was also important for hunting and fighting in wars. A horse who is hard to control or <u>flighty</u> could cost his owner his life. For example, a horse who spooks at a deer is not one you'd want to take hunting. You wouldn't be able to get close enough to your prey to kill it.

It's true that most horses can be trained, but the Nez Percé wanted their horses to have abilities of their own. Horses had to have a willingness to learn and be capable of developing loyal relationships. In one generation (about 20 years), the courageous Nez Percé became excellent horse people. It is written that the Nez Percé could ride bareback at full speed across rough countryside while firing bows and arrows.

The spotted horses whom the Nez Percé liked so much came to be called Palousa, and finally they were named as we know them today—Appaloosa. The name is new; the breed is not. In fact, the breed can be traced back to 100 B.C. in China, where it was called the Heavenly Horse.

The Native American and His War Pony

Although most tribes did not corral or otherwise contain their horses, there was one exception: the war pony. Although a horse, it was called a pony by the French and English who were comparing the smaller war pony to their own huge draft horses[2] who were bred to pull heavy wagons. Most Native warriors kept their ponies tied or hobbled[3] close to the lodge at all times. Some warriors would even

▶ How did warriors treat their war ponies?

---

2. **draft horses.** Large and very strong horses often used for pulling loads
3. **hobbled.** Fastened by the legs to prevent from straying

---

words for everyday use

flight • y (flī´tē) *adj.*, lacking stability or steadiness. *The flighty server couldn't decide whether to bring us the bill or another glass of milk.*

bring their ponies into the lodge during bad weather, forcing the women and children to sleep elsewhere. Sometimes when a warrior died, his war pony would be put to death alongside him as a sacrifice. Or sometimes when a horse was lost in war, the warrior would make a wooden sculpture of the horse and paint on the wounds that had killed him.

The war pony was chosen for his speed, <u>agility</u>, surefootedness, sensibility, endurance, and dependability. But above all, the pony was chosen for his <u>temperament</u>. The war pony had to have nerves of steel and the sense to "catch" a rider who had lost his balance. The pony needed unbridled speed and the ability to stand silently until led to do otherwise. More than anything, the war pony needed to be reliable. Mistakes in war meant lives lost.

◄ What were war ponies like?

Once they began to use and depend on horses, Native riders realized that their success and even their survival depended on the relationship they built with their horses. Native Americans knew that an understanding and strong relationship between human and horse is what builds reliability.

A warrior's ability to communicate with his horse was one of the most valuable skills he could develop. Children began to learn about horses at a young age. Two-year-olds were placed on a gentle horse and tied in the saddle. A six-year-old might get his own pony from his father or grandfather. By that age, he could already help herd the horses. Older boys competed in races and riding contests. They showed off their skill by hanging off the side of a galloping horse and scooping an object off the ground.

War ponies were trained by their riders, sometimes over many years. Looking back, we may think that in those days people had more time to work with their horses. Not true. They put in 16 to 18 hours of work each day to ensure their survival. Their work included hunting, cooking, cleaning, tanning hides,

◄ Who trained war ponies?

words for everyday use	**agil • i • ty** (ə ji´ lə tē) *n.*, ability to move with quick easy grace. *I was amazed at the <u>agility</u> of the hurdlers at the track meet.*	**tem • per • a • ment** (tem´pə rə ment) *n.*, characteristic or habitual inclination or mode of emotional response. *My father dislikes speaking in front of large groups because he has a nervous <u>temperament</u>.*

gathering nuts, berries, roots, and herbs. If you spend all day at school and play sports afterward, you probably have twice as much time left over for a horse than did the average Native American. But those horsemen understood that without a healthy working relationship with their horses, they had better not go to war.

The war pony was companion, best friend, soul mate, and teacher to the Native rider. Most important, the war pony was *kola:* a friend with whom you could face many enemies. The word *kola* is not normally used to describe animals but is reserved for human brother-warriors. In using *kola* to describe their relationship to their horses, Native American warriors are saying their horses are equals as brother-warriors.

▶ *What is a* kola?

Badge of Honor, Declaration of Courage

▶ *Why did Native Americans paint their horses?*

Native Americans painted their horses with special symbolic paints to intimidate the enemy, give their horses strength and courage in battle, and advertise the achievements of both rider and horse.

The medicine paint was made with natural ingredients: ash for white or gray; charcoal for black; berries for reds, blues, and purples; ocher[4] for yellow. These ingredients were blended with either water or animal fat to make paint. The Plains warriors often painted the same symbols on themselves as they did on the flanks and necks of their horses. War paint was a badge or medal that indicated particular accomplishments, just like the badges you earn as a Girl or Boy Scout. Each symbol on the horse had its own meaning that was known to all members of the horse culture. A circle placed around the eye of the horse served to give the horse better vision. Upside down horseshoes indicated how many horse raids the rider had participated in. A design shaped like a keyhole placed on the horse by a medicine person or spiritual leader was a blessing and protector. Handprints indicated the number of enemies killed

▶ *What did the symbols painted on a horse mean?*

---

4. **ocher.** Red or yellow and often impure iron ore used as a pigment

by the rider in hand-to-hand combat without the aid of weapons. Stacked horizontal lines counted *coup.*

Coup, a French word meaning touch, was a way of dishonoring the enemy by touching him. The belief that a warrior could obtain some of the soul of his enemy, as well as some of his strength, courage, and energy, motivated warriors to count coup whenever the opportunity arose. Coup did not always precede the death of the enemy but was sometimes used as a warning to the enemy to get out of tribal territory.

◀ *What does* coup *mean?*

Native Americans also wove things into their war ponies' manes and tails. A lock of the rider's own hair was tied into the mane of his pony so their spirits could be one. A feather from a hawk, eagle, or falcon (all considered to be war birds) gave the horse the speed and agility of that bird. Hail marks, made famous by the Oglada Lakota warrior Crazy Horse, were believed to give the horse and rider the strength and fury of a great hail storm.

By being a partner with humans, the horse achieved a special status and was no longer a hunted animal.

Critical Thinking

1. Why did some Native Americans consider the war pony a *kola,* or a friend with whom you could face many enemies?
2. Why were horses once so important to Native Americans? Why have things changed between Native Americans and horses? What might remain the same?

Creative Writing Activities

Advice Column

Pretend that you are an advice columnist and that three characters in *High Elk's Treasure* have written to you for advice. First write the letters from the characters to you, the advice columnist. Then give the characters advice or suggestions for solving their problems. Explain why you believe each character should respond in a particular way.

Continue the Story

Continue the story of *High Elk's Treasure* by writing another chapter. What do the High Elks do with the treasure they've found? What more do they learn about how their great-grandfather started his herd? What do they discover about what happened at the Battle of Little Big Horn? As you construct your chapter, include dialogue between characters. Refer to the definition of *dialogue* in the Handbook of Literary Terms for more information. Use dialogue in the novel as a guide for adding punctuation and quotation marks.

Newspaper Front Page

Look at the front page of several newspapers you get at home or at school. Make your own front page of a newspaper and fill it with stories about the exciting events that occur in *High Elk's Treasure*. One of the stories should be your headline story. Add pictures to some of the stories. Continue some of the stories on additional pages.

Play

Write a play that is set in a radio or television studio that is reporting on events that happen in *High Elk's Treasure* before, during, and after the severe weather watch. Include such things as updates the station receives from its field reporters on what is happening at the school, near the creek, and at the High

Elk ranch. You might also include live interviews with Mr. Gray Bear, Grandma, and Joe's parents.

Poetry Booklet

Write three poems about relatives in your family. Use your five senses to find ways to describe each person. Make a list of what you see, hear, feel, taste, and smell when you think of each person before you begin. Include this list with your project. When you are finished with your poems, create a cover for your booklet and decorate the pages of your booklet with pictures or designs.

Personal Response

Choose a person or event in *High Elk's Treasure* that reminds you of a person or event in your own life. Why are you reminded of that person or event? Tell how Sneve describes the person or event in the novel. Then tell us about the person or event from your own life. Possible events and people include: the storm, finding a treasure, running away from home, helpful neighbors, Joe's grandmother, Howard, or Mr. Blue Shield.

Yearbook

Predict what three major characters and three minor characters will be doing a year from now. Then create a yearbook, or a record of what the characters do the year after Otokahe is born. Use details and information from *High Elk's Treasure* to support your predictions. Illustrate your yearbook.

Critical Writing Activities

The following topics are suitable for short critical essays on *High Elk's Treasure*. An essay written on one of these topics should begin with an introductory paragraph that states the thesis, or main idea, of the essay. The introductory paragraph should be followed by several paragraphs that support the thesis, using examples from the novel. The essay should conclude with a paragraph that summarizes the points made in the body of the essay and that reinforces the thesis.

Comparing and Contrasting Literature

Compare and contrast things you learn about growing up in *High Elk's Treasure* to what you learn about growing up in the selection from *Completing the Circle*. Start by identifying what you learn about growing up in each one. Organize your thoughts into a Venn diagram like the one below. Note similarities you find in the two works in the center where the two circles join. Note differences you find in each work in the parts of the circle outside the intersection of the two circles. Use your Venn diagram to develop a thesis for your first introductory paragraph. The body of your essay should support your thesis with evidence from each work. Then write a final paragraph that concludes your comparison of the two works.

Growing Up

High Elk's Treasure   *Completing the Circle*

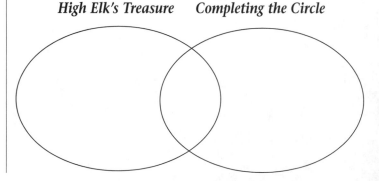

Building Suspense

High Elk's Treasure has several exciting events that build suspense. Identify these events. Then examine how the author builds suspense in each event. What complicates each event? How do the characters handle the event? What do the characters do right and what do they do wrong in handling the event? How is the suspense resolved?

Theme—Heritage Is Important

Throughout *High Elk's Treasure* and in each of the related readings, the authors refer to the importance of one's heritage. How do the authors of these readings show the pride that people take in their heritage? What interests and goals of real and fictional characters are passed along from generation to generation? How has your heritage affected your goals? How is your heritage the same as or different from those you have read about? How can you learn more about your heritage?

Motive

What motivates Mr. Blue Shield to help the High Elks? In what ways does Mr. Blue Shield help the High Elks? Why is his help so necessary? Why do others help the High Elks? Consider Howard, Dr. Scott, and Mr. Iron Cloud in your response.

Prediction

What predictions did you make about the treasure in *High Elk's Treasure* as you read? What predictions did you make about the treasure at these points in your reading: before reading, after the first chapter, after Joe found the bundle, and after the bundle was opened. Explain why you made the predictions that you did.

Projects

Your Family's Treasures

Talk to your parents, grandparents, and other relatives about objects and stories that have been passed down from generation to generation. Draw pictures or take photographs of objects that are important to your family. How has the object been handed down? Why is it important to your family? How is the object cared for? What are some customs that your family follows at important celebrations? Have some of the customs changed over the years? In what ways? Include a family tree and maps showing how your ancestors moved around the country or the world.

Interview

Interview an older person in your family. Write questions you want to ask before the interview begins. You may use a video recorder, a cassette recorder, or a pencil to record what the person tells you about your family's history and customs. Then create a written, audio, or video version of the interview.

Internet Research Project

Research one of the following topics on the Internet. Good websites to use are included with each topic. Note that Internet sites often change and that you may need to do your own search using appropriate key words.

 a. How to preserve treasures from the past:
 - http://www.slv.vic.gov.au/slv/conservation/conserve.htm
 - http://www.myhistory.org/saving
 - http://www.imls.gov/closer/archive/hlt_m0600.htm

 Or search Internet encyclopedias such as Encarta or Britannica using key words "art preservation" or "art conservation."
 b. What happened at the Battle of Little Big Horn:
 - http://www.nps.gov/libi/Sioux.html

- http://www.thehistorynet.com/wildwest/
  articles/06962_text.htm
- http://ibiscom.com/custer.htm

Or search Internet encyclopedias using key words "Little Big Horn" or "George Custer."

c. Efforts to save wild horses in the West:
  - http://www.pbs.org/wildhorses
  - http://www.savewildhorses.org
  - http://www.wildhorsesanctuary.org

d. Rock art, stone pictographs found on rocks and caves around the world:
  - http://www.tmm.utexas.edu/anthro/rockart/
    index.html
  - http://perth.uwlax.edu/mvac/pastcultures/
    rock%20art/rock%20art.htm
  - http://www.public.asu.edu/aznha/palatki/
    aboutpal.htm
  - http://www.nps.gov/petr/

Use at least two Internet sites as you conduct your research. After you complete your research, create a poster that illustrates what you learned. Your poster should have a title, information written in your own words, and pictures or diagrams that help explain your topic. Present your poster to the class.

Picture Book Plot Development

Create a picture book that can be read to younger children that retells the sequence of events in *High Elk's Treasure*. Your book should include a cover, title page, story pages, and a back cover with information about the author of the book, Virginia Driving Hawk Sneve.

Map

Create a three-dimensional map that shows the buildings, creeks, peaks, and other features found on the High Elk Range. You will need to build the structures and land forms. Add notes to your map that describe what took place at each location.

Glossary of Words for Everyday Use

Pronunciation Key

Vowel Sounds

a	hat	ō	go	ə	extra
ā	play	ȯ	paw, born		under
ä	star	u̇	book, put		civil
e	then	ü	blue, stew		honor
ē	me	oi	boy		bogus
i	sit	ou	wow		burn
ī	my	u	up		

Consonant Sounds

b	but	l	lip	t	sit
ch	watch	m	money	th	with
d	do	n	on	v	valley
f	fudge	ŋ	song, sink	w	work
g	go	p	pop	y	yell
h	hot	r	rod	z	pleasure
j	jump	s	see		
k	brick	sh	she		

ag • gra • va • tion (a grə vā´ shən) *n.*, act or circumstance that intensifies or makes worse

ag • i • ta • tion (aj ə tā´ shən) *n.*, emotional disturbance

ag • ile (a´ jəl) *adj.*, able to move in a quick and easy fashion

agil • i • ty (ə ji´ lə tē) *n.*, ability to move with quick easy grace

au • then • tic (ə then´ tik) *adj.*, not false or imitation

au • thor • i • ta • tive (ə thȯr´ ə tā tiv) *adj.*, having or proceeding from authority; official

bar • ren (bar´ ən) *adj.*, producing little or no vegetation

bel • lig • er • ent (bə lij´ rənt) *adj.*, inclined to or exhibiting assertiveness, hostility, or combativeness. **belligerently,** *adv.*

bri • dle (brī´ dəl) *v.*, put on the headgear with which a horse is governed and which carries a bit and reins

brunt (brənt´) *n.*, principal force, shock, or stress

buck • skin (bək´ skin) *n.*, skin of a male deer

bum (bəm´) *v.*, obtain by begging

can • ter (kan´ tər) *n.*, three-beat gait resembling but smoother and slower than the gallop

cap • tiv • i • ty (kap tiv´ və tē) *n.*, state of being captive

car • go (kär´ gō) *n.,* goods or merchandise conveyed in a ship, airplane, or vehicle

con • sol • i • date (kənsä´ lə dāt) *v.,* join together in one whole

cor • ral (kə ral´) *n.,* pen or enclosure for confining or capturing livestock

cor • sage (kȯr säzh´) *n.,* arrangement of flowers worn as a fashion accessory

coun • te • nance (kaunt´ ən ənts) *n.,* face, or visage, especially the face as an indication of mood, emotion, or character

croon (krūn´) *v.,* speak or sing in a gentle murmuring manner

deb • u • tante (deb´ yu̇ tänt) *n.,* young woman making a formal entrance into society

de • bris (de brē´) *n.,* scattered remains of something broken or destroyed

des • e • crate (de´ si krāt) *v.,* violate the sanctity of

des • per • ate (des´ pər it) *adj.,* suffering extreme need or anxiety. **desperately,** *adv.*

di • a • lect (dī´ ə lekt) *n.,* regional variety of a language distinguished by unique vocabulary, grammar, or pronunciation

dis • cern (di sern´) *v.,* recognize or identify as separate and distinct. **discernible,** *adj.*

do • mes • ti • cate (də mes´ ti kāt) *v.,* adapt an animal or plant to life in intimate association with and to the advantage of humans

em • i • grant (e´ mi grənt) *n.,* departing or having departed from a country to settle elsewhere

en • fran • chise (in fran´ chīz) *v.,* give full privileges of citizenship to; especially to give the right to vote

en • route (än rüt´) *adv.,* on or along the way

en • thrall (in thrȯl´) *v.,* hold by or as if by a spell

en • vel • op (in ve´ ləp) *v.,* enclose or enfold completely as if with a covering

fledg • ling (flej´ liŋ) *n.,* one that is new

flight • y (flī´ tē) *adj.,* lacking stability or steadiness

folk • lore (fō´ klōr) *n.,* traditional customs, sayings, tales, dances, or art forms preserved among a people

fore • stall (fōr stȯl´) *v.,* get ahead of; prevent

forge (fōrj´) *v.,* make or imitate falsely

fu • tile (fyü´ təl) *adj.,* completely ineffective. **futilely,** *adv.*

gid • dy (gi´ dē) *adj.,* mad, foolish

gouge (gauj´) *v.*, scoop out with or as if with a gouge

heir • loom (ar´ lūm) *n.*, piece of property that descends to the heir as part of an inheritance of property

her • i • tage (her´ ə tij) *n.*, something transmitted by or acquired from a predecessor

his • to • ri • an (hi stōr´ ē ən) *n.*, student or writer of history

home • stead (hōm´ sted) *n.*, home and adjoining land occupied by a family

il • lu • mi • nate (i lü´ mə nāt) *v.*, brighten with light

im • mi • grant (i´ mi grənt) *n.*, person who comes to a country to take up permanent residence

im • prov • i • sa • tion (im präv ə zā´ shən) *n.*, act of composing, reciting, or singing without preparation

le • ni • ent (lē´ nē ənt) *adj.*, exerting a soothing or easing influence

lib • er • ate (li´ bə rāt) *v.*, set free

lunge (lənj´) *v.*, sudden forward thrust or reach

man • ger (mān´ jər) *n.*, trough or open box in a stable designed to hold feed or fodder for livestock

mar • vel (mär´ vəl) *v.*, become filled with surprise or wonder

mea • ger (mē´ gər) *adj.*, deficient in quantity

mem • o • ra • bil • ia (me mə rə bi´ lē ə) *n.*, things that are remarkable and worthy of remembrance

mo • bile (mō´ bil) *adj.*, capable of moving or being moved. **mobility,** *n.*

mus • ty (məs´ tē) *adj.*, smelling of damp and decay

muse (myüz´) *v.*, become absorbed in thought

no • mad • ic (nō ma´ dik) *adj.*, roaming about from place to place aimlessly, frequently, or without a pattern

no • tor • i • ous (nō tōr´ ē əs) *adj.*, generally known and talked of

nos • tal • gia (nä stal´ jə) *n.*, longing for something past

ob • long (ä´ bloŋ) *adj.*, deviating from a square, circular, or spherical form by elongation in one dimension

pal • o • mi • no (pal ə mē´ nō) *n.*, horse that is pale cream or gold in color and has a flaxen or white mane and tail

par • ti • tion (pär ti´ shən) *n.*, something that divides, such as an interior dividing wall

peer (pir´) *v.*, look narrowly or curiously

pom • pous (pöm´ pəs) *adj.*, excessively elevated or ornate

pre • his • tor • ic (prē his tōr´ ik) *adj.,* of or existing in times before written history

pre • vail (pri vāl´) *v.,* be frequent. **prevailing,** *adj.*

prec • i • pice (pre´sə pəs) *n.,* very steep or overhanging place

pred • a • tor (pre´ də tər) *n.,* one that preys, destroys, or devours

pun • gent (pən´ jənt) *adj.,* causing a sharp or irritating sensation

raw • hide (ro´ hīd) *n.,* untanned cattle skin

re • luc • tant (ri lək´ tənt) *adj.,* feeling or showing aversion, hesitation, or unwillingness. **reluctantly,** *adv.*

re • morse (ri mors´) *n.,* gnawing distress arising from a sense of guilt for past wrongs

rem • i • ni • scen • ce (re mə ni´ sənts) *n.,* remembrance of a long-forgotten experience or fact

rev • er • ent (rev´ rənt) *adj.,* expressing or characterizing honor or respect. **reverently,** *adv.*

rit • u • al (ri´ chə wəl) *n.,* customarily repeated

rus • tle (rə´ səl) *v.,* steal cattle

shy (shī´) *v.,* start suddenly aside through fright or alarm

sou • ven • ir (sū və nir´) *n.,* something that serves as a reminder

spec • u • late (spe´ kyə lāt) *v.,* meditate or ponder on a subject

sprad • dle (spra´ dəl) *v.,* sprawl

staunch (stonch´) *adj.,* steadfast in loyalty or principle

stir • rup (stər´ əp) *n.,* one of a pair of frames attached to a saddle for the rider's feet

stock (stäk´) *n.,* all of the animals kept or raised on a farm; livestock

taut (tot´) *adj.,* having no give or slack

tem • per • a • ment (tem´ pə rə ment) *n.,* characteristic or habitual inclination or mode of emotional response

teth • er (te´ thər) *v.,* fasten or restrain by or as if by a tether

thun • der • head (thən´ dər hed) *n.,* rounded mass of cumulus clouds often appearing before a thunderstorm

trough (trof´) *n.,* long, shallow, often V-shaped receptacle for the drinking water or feed of domestic animals

vex (veks´) *v.,* irritate or annoy by petty provocations

wrench (rench´) *n.,* sudden tug at one's emotions. **wrenching,** *adj.*

Handbook of Literary Terms

Character. A **character** is a person or animal who takes part in the action of a literary work. Characters can be classified as *major characters* or *minor characters*. **Major characters** are ones who play important roles in a work. **Minor characters** are ones who play less important roles.

Conflict. A **conflict** is a struggle between two people or things in a literary work. This struggle can be internal or external. A struggle that takes place between a character and some outside force such as another character or nature is called an *external conflict.* A struggle that takes place within a character is called an *internal conflict.*

Dialogue. Dialogue is conversation involving two or more people or characters.

Legend. A **legend** is a story coming down from the past, often based on important real events or characters.

Motive. Motive is a reason for acting in a certain way.

Oral Tradition. An **oral tradition** encompasses the works, ideas, or customs of a culture, passed by word of mouth from generation to generation.

Plot. A **plot** is a series of events related to a central conflict, or struggle. A plot usually involves the introduction of a conflict, its development, and its eventual resolution. The following terms are used to describe the parts of a plot:

• The *exposition,* or introduction, sets the tone or mood, introduces the characters and the setting, and provides necessary background information.

• The *inciting incident* is the event that introduces the central conflict.

• The *climax* is the high point of interest or suspense in the story.

• The *resolution* is the point at which the central conflict is ended, or resolved.

• The *dénouement* is any material that follows the resolution and that ties up loose ends. Note that some plots do not contain all of these parts.

Point of View. **Point of view** is the vantage point from which a story is told. If a story is told from the *first-person point of view,* the narrator uses the pronouns *I* and *we* and is a part of or a witness to the action. When a story is told from a *third-person point of view,* the narrator is outside the action; uses words such as *he, she, it,* and *they*; and avoids the use of *I* and *we.*

Protagonist. A **protagonist** is the main character in a story. The protagonist faces a struggle or conflict.

Setting. The **setting** of a literary work is the time and place in which it happens.

Suspense. Suspense is a feeling of expectation, anxiousness, or curiosity. Writers create suspense by raising questions in the reader's mind and by using details that create strong emotions. Suspense works the plot toward the *climax,* or the point of highest interest in a literary work.

Theme. A **theme** is a central idea in a literary work. It is often found by looking for the meaning behind the things that happen in a story. You usually won't find the theme actually stated in the story, and often a story has more than one theme.

Acknowledgments

BowTie™ Press. *Out of the Saddle: Native American Horsemanship™* by GaWaNi Pony Boy. Copyright ©1998 by BowTie™ Press. All rights reserved.

Virginia Driving Hawk Sneve. "I Watched an Eagle Soar" by Virginia Driving Hawk Sneve. ©Virginia Driving Hawk Sneve. Reprinted by permission of the author.

The Greenfield Review Press. "Looking for My Old Indian Grandmother in the Summer Heat of 1980" by Diane Glancy. Copyright ©1983 *The Greenfield Review Press.* Reprinted by permission of the author.

Houghton Mifflin Company. "Family Treasures, Family Pleasures" by Lila Perl from *The Great Ancestor Hunt: The Fun of Finding Out Who You Are.* Text copyright ©1989 by Lila Perl. Reprinted by permission of Clarion Books/Houghton Mifflin Company. All rights reserved.

University of Nebraska Press. Reprinted from *Completing the Circle* by Virginia Driving Hawk Sneve by permission of the University of Nebraska Press. ©1995 by the University of Nebraska Press.

Ray A. Young Bear. "grandmother" by Ray A. Young Bear from *Winter of the Salamander.* ©Ray A. Young Bear. Reprinted by permission of the author.